BONAVENTURE

by

Larry Rochelle

This book is a work of fiction. Names, characters, places and incidents are products of the author's imagination or are used fictitiously.

Lulu Press   Published by Larry Rochelle
Pittsboro, North Carolina   September 11, 2011
ISBN 978-1-257-83345-0

For Liz and the PT staff at the Duke Center:

Thank you for getting me up and walking again!

There is a tendency to simplify the culprits, such as trying to blame the C.I.A. alone for the Watergate affair, or other political assassinations and conspiracies. The fact is that the Pentagon, all branches of the armed forces and the combined intelligence agencies work together in these plots. Extermination, murder, brain mutilation, electrode implants, and torture are nothing but a continuation of policies begun in Nazi Germany and imported into the United States during World War II.

---Mae Brussell

BONAVENTURE

1

Recovering

It's no fun being dead.

And after two weeks in a coma at Durham Hospital, Palmer Morel decided to wake up. His blue eyes would not open at first. His willpower was disengaged and he craved much more sleep.

But there was this urgent voice, this voice pleading, saying over and over, *you can do it, you can do it.*

So he woke up.

***

The urgent note came by courier, or should it more accurately be said, by a so-called recovering, knee-replacement patient. While Andrea York, DPT, sat in her therapy office, writing about his progress, Steven "Sleepy" Knorr limped next to her, bent over carefully and placed a sealed manila envelope onto her notepad.

Andrea looked up slowly. She knew what the envelope contained. Frowning, she lifted it off the notepad and slid it into her green carry-all next to the desk.

"Thanks," was all she said. Sleepy, her former patient, turned and limped away, down the hall, past the check-in desk and then out into the bright parking lot.

The Deerington Health Center lot was filled with cars on this warm afternoon. He found his silver Prius, struggled to get his right leg inside and drove carefully out the entrance onto 15/501 highway.

Now, he thought, back at Fort Bragg they'd all find out just how good young Andrea York really was.

***

There was no immediate pain that first day of sensibility, no tightness, no fear. Morel smiled at the nurses who took his vitals. The nurses explained the dripping of drugs into his arm, controlled by the device he held in his right hand. More pain, you click for more juice. Simple. Pain gone. Morel nodded. Smiled.

But they warned him the juice would be turned to a lower setting each day. *Don't want you to become an addict*, they explained.

And then the pain did come back after lunch, after the consommé, the cold grape Popsicle, the check of his blood pressure, 128 over 80. It began with a dull ache in his head, then a tightening in his back where the stitches were, and when he moved, a surprising yank in his belly where the tree limb in the Haw River had grazed his kidney and now caused him to cry out, "Nurse!"

***

Leafing through the folder, Andrea looked at Palmer Morel's dossier photos carefully. A tennis player. A big blond, blue-eyed tennis player. Cute, smiling at some kids he was teaching. Another photo of him holding up an old Jack Kramer tennis racquet. A newspaper photo of him and his doubles partner winning a tournament in Memphis. A b/w headshot from his own resume'. A list of strange acting-out episodes Morel was involved in during the last five years: Kansas City, Toledo, New Orleans, Nashville, Durham. Some photos of his various women friends taken from afar, long-lens photos. Blondes, brunettes, redheads, Asians. Quite a variety.

Then she picked out a few photos of his child, nicknamed TJ, aka Tony Jack (TJ) Morel. Feisty kid, playing with toy trains, laughing, riding on Morel's shoulders at a parade. Swinging a small tennis racquet. Rolling yellow tennis balls on the floor with his dad.

Then she read parts of the FBI report on the shooting near the Haw River. A disputed confrontation. Action instigated after some confidential complaints from right-wing citizens. A long report from an ex-military man at Fearrington Village. Photos of the swollen river on the day of the shooting. A photo of the crowd gathered on the Haw River bridge, all of the citizens looking for his body as he was swept away. A color photo of Morel's latest girl, a redhead, Cat Gallaher, crying, holding TJ as she crossed the Haw River bridge after the shooting.

Andrea pondered. *Shit. How did Morel get involved in all of this terrorist activity? He seems so normal.*

***

Morel had just one visitor during his entire recovery, a young, lovely, Asian woman who parked her Karmann Ghia blocks away from the hospital and fled quickly into the brick apartment house nearby. After ten minutes she always left by the back entrance, down some steps and into the waiting, dark-blue car, a 2002 Grand Prix with a Chatham county license plate. The driver was an admiring, older male student taking her pottery course in Siler City.

Within a few minutes she would get out of the car behind the hospital, and, taking a short zigzag jog through a parking lot, she would enter the intensive care wing. The car would wait one hour until she returned.

She would take Palmer Morel's hand during the visit. She had saved him as he was barely breathing after falling into the Haw River. She had fished him out near the old bridge in Bynum. She had wrapped him in a thin blanket, somehow stuffed him in the back of her Karmann Ghia and drove him to UNC.

The ER crew had at first thought he was dead he was so blue. And to the rest of the world, he was.

Only the Asian potter from Savannah, Sara Jensen, had believed he must have survived the fall into the Haw River, then searched for him and saved him.

***

Secrecy suited Andrea York. Since grad school, she had led a double life, working by day as a physical therapist at the Rehab Center in Deerington Village, working extra hours at night for the government when needed as part of a secretive black ops unit from Fort Bragg.

Nearing her thirtieth birthday, Andrea was often stressed by her dual role, the long hours with patients recovering from knee and hip replacement, the drudgery of the Medicare paperwork that kept her at work after hours to finish.

Then, after a quick supper, she usually needed to log in on her computer at the Fort Bragg website, getting assignments to accost suspected terrorists at the bars in Chapel Hill, Raleigh and Durham. And nearly every evening, she'd take off her drab green work clothes, change into her bright, party clothes, showing her breasts, her legs, enticing dangerous men from middle-east countries so that she could discover their secrets, taking them dancing in Raleigh.

But now she had a new assignment: one with more stability she hoped. She was to get a special patient, one being watched by black ops, a person who had been shot through and through his shoulder but who had somehow survived. Tennis pro Palmer Morel was being treated at the UNC Hospital but would be moved tonight to a small, seldom-used therapy room under the steps at her Deerington Health Care Center where she worked. It would be Andrea's task to watch him, listen to him, and kill him if ordered.

Pushing her long back hair behind her ear, she opened the brown folder again. Left inside was a smaller envelope. She counted five glass capsules inside, noted the three long hat pins and quickly shut the envelope. She knew she could use these if she had to.

***

A week or so later at UNC, after another of Morel's bland lunches, Sara brought out a packet wrapped in string, an unsightly package of paper, some pages ripped, most pages turning brown.

"This is what your dad sent you yesterday. He thinks it might help." Sara slowly took off the string and gave the sleepy Morel the first page.

He took it with his left hand and held it up to the gray light coming through the little hospital window. It was an old letter sent to his dad, James Morel, from the United States Congress dated February 5, 1975. Morel shook his head slightly in annoyance. His dad had been a real conspiracy nut back in the day.

***

Of course, Morel vaguely remembered his dad's letters from those congressmen in the late 1970s. His dad had been eager to see justice in the John Kennedy assassination accomplished. He had written letters wildly into the night, posting them early the next day, and then waiting for weeks until he got a reply.

Some of the letters he got back were formulaic, cold, distant, letters prepared ahead of time to send to those citizens upset by the assassination. Other letters turned up unexpectedly; they were blunt, honest, with emotion. These good letters he would show his ten-year-old son, Palmer, who had been fascinated at the time by the history, the letterheads, the signatures of Bill Gradison, Henry Gonzalez and others.

But now his dad sent the same letters to Palmer, in hopes of clarifying a similar ugly mood in America after the Obama election. There was assassination in the air again. Mr. Morel hoped these letters that might help explain to Palmer why he had been shot at the Haw River.

His dad argued these right-wing assassinations changed the course of history, even though some might argue one man does not make much difference. But the country changed big after Kennedy's death, and the Warren Commission cover-up was despicable, many Commission members being military men, CIA men, hating Kennedy's politics or fired by Kennedy after they had sponsored assassinations abroad and planned the assassination of Fidel Castro.

His dad got really upset in 1978 when the country took a serious look at Kennedy's murder, and even then it was tough to get any money from the Republicans in Congress, tough to get subpoena power to question the suspects before they disappeared or got dumped in the sea off Miami Beach, like Johnny Roselli.

And these Hearings hadn't stopped the assassination mentality of the military, the CIA, the FBI and the other secret services. Now they had drones and electronics to kill from a distance, Mr. Morel would argue.

These new right-wing boys didn't have to pick off a president from a tall building any more. No. Now they could get him anywhere. They could use roadside bombs as they had used near Fort Bragg, trying to kill Obama last fall. And if that didn't work, they could pick off their enemies near the Haw River Bridge using telescopic sights from a helicopter, as they had tried with Morel recently. No wonder Palmer felt the cold shiver of fear again, the pain in his back throbbing in remembrance.

So, his dad warned Morel to worry all over again, *Will they come and get me in the hospital? Can I trust the nurses, the maintenance crew?*

***

Morel dozed off, his long legs leaning over the edge of the little hospital bed. His mind was confused, dealing with past and present horrors. One of his oxycontin dreams began to churn:

Confront, confront, you gotta confront. No one else seems reliable. The paper cutters were working and down the sides of the chair the pile was growing. Mostly Democrats replied. The Republicans gathered, yes, but were snapping the scissors, cutting up the letters, the attempts at justice. And JFK was there, sifting through the mounds, and Bobby and Martin, like garbage men they were. Putting everything in black bags. But Palmer and his dad stopped them. "Open those sacks of letters. Open and see the answers." Then the mushroom cloud started small just outside Cuba on a colorful map, and oil began to flow while a brown tornado blew across the Keys, Morel covered his head in a pillow until it was gone. Only the mushroom remained, small but growing, and Mr. James Morel reached down, plucked up the mushroom and popped it into his mouth.

***

In charge of safety, the Governor of North Carolina was worried about the effectiveness of the NC Highway Patrol. After suffering through a series of scandals, troopers were fired for having sex with prisoners in the backseats of their cruisers, getting it on with other troopers' wives, harassing female drivers stopped for speeding, and hooking up with prostitutes.

So, the Governor had appointed a new Highway Patrol Commander; and Colonel Max Melty had seen enough. His stocky body and gray hair demanded respect, but his florid red face sometimes strained credulity. His anger was strangely palpable and his fuse was short. As he shouted from the podium, people wondered about his own integrity and sanity.

At his first press conference in Chapel Hill, he quickly announced the firing of six troopers and asserted that the sex investigation was continuing. His downturned, grim mouth sneered in frustration and he refused to take any questions.

But as Melty walked away from the mic and down some steps to his right, a young male reporter from the NEWS & OBSERVER shouted out a question anyway: "Colonel, how's the investigation into the Palmer Morel shooting going? Have you found his body yet?"

That got Melty's attention. He stomped back up the stairs to the mic, very angry now, veins pulsing, targeting the reporter with his withering stare. "Now don't you fault us with that. We put in over a thousand man-hours dredging the Haw River, checking along the banks under dangerous conditions. That body could be in the Atlantic Ocean. You all saw how high the Haw was that day, how fast it was moving. You all know that body could be anywhere. Just get the heck outta my face on that one, boys. We done our job."

He moved away again, but returned to the podium abruptly. "And don't have no pity on Morel or his lonely girl friend or his baby son," he shouted. "That man was a traitor and deserved what he got."

The Colonel stepped away again, grunted and thought back to a previous month when a call came from Fort Bragg, an urgent call to track down Palmer Morel, an order he, as the NC Director of Special Ops, helped carry out with dispatch, ending with Morel's big splash into the Haw River north of Pittsboro. He smiled. He had done his job. And Morel was gone. Good. One less liberal to fuck up the United States.

***

Palmer's little boy, TJ, was bewildered, upset, not fully understanding at all. His shaggy blond hair and light blue eyes reflected his dad's, his strong jaw line was firm, his lips pouting. His dad was missing, and his two-year-old life was crammed with disturbing events: police officers, helicopters, news reporters, a sense of being rushed, always being yanked away from his toys, and from his normal activities.

He played quietly now with his Thomas the Train set, pushing the engines one after another down the long, polished hallway toward the front porch of the town home in Deerington Village. The colorful engines Gordon, Toby, Emily and Henry puffed their way down the golden, sunlit floor one at a time, while TJ tried to invent a new story line for their adventures.

But he couldn't. His mind flitted here and there, remembering his dad's face, his smile, and wanting his dad to come home. Sitting down, he grabbed his own little bare feet and paused in thought, rocking, rocking for comfort.

"Where Daddy," he whispered. Then, he threw Thomas his favorite train across the floor, hopped up and ran back to the kitchen where his dad's girl, the redhead, Cat Gallaher, was making lunch.

Grilled cheese and tomato sandwiches were on the front burner of the stove, red fruit punch was poured out in plastic glasses at the table. Cat could hear TJ's little feet scampering down the hallway toward her. She stood near the kitchen entrance and watched TJ plummet toward her bare legs.

Stopping abruptly, he looked straight up into her eyes. "Daddy?" he asked.

Cat swept him up and carried him to the sunroom, showing him the bright leaves of autumn, the reds, the yellows, and the orange glory out the wide window. Her voice cried out, "Daddy, help me, help me, please!"

Cat laughed, "Remember, TJ, I told you Daddy had been part of nature. Like Superman. He can see you. Look. Up in the blue sky. He watches you. He loves you. But guess what? I just found out he's not in the beautiful sky at all any more."

TJ listened, and then muttered, "Whaa? In sky? No?"

"No, TJ, he came down to earth again. He's not gone up to heaven. He's gonna visit us this afternoon!"

2

Suspicions

Sara let Morel sleep. His body was recovering, and he needed the sleep. As the pain pills relaxed him, he simply gave in to rest.

She had seen the anger as Morel's eyes had scanned the Senator's note, the first in another series of correspondence his father had collected during the government's late 1970s investigation of the 1960s right-wing assassinations of Kennedy, King, and Kennedy.

She fingered her little tiger pendant, a juju toy reminding her of her college, the Savannah State Tigers, and she watched as Morel stirred, then gave her a sleepy smile.

He touched her hand and then reached for another letter from his dad, scanning it through his sleepy eyes. She pulled her chair closer to the hospital bed. "Find any answers while you were sleeping, Palmer?'

"Well, nothing new," he yawned. "Dad kept these letters in his roll top desk in his front office near the parlor when we lived briefly in Cincinnati. He read them and scattered them on the floor. I was like ten-years-old, in grade school. I remember he was very upset then. Angry about the military control of our country. Very political guy.

Always writing to Congress. Wanting them to get JFK's killers. He blamed the military."

Morel could envision his dad then, a young father intensely following the Hearings on TV, yelling at the screen, wanting the cover-up of the JFK murder to be unraveled at last. His dad felt like part of the investigation, writing his letters, getting notes from the powerful. But, in the end, the committee and the lack of arrests in the case disappointed him badly.

So, he changed, turning instead to his son for meaning, connection. He started to push Palmer to practice more tennis. Re-focused on his family, trying to forget assassination plots. What good could one person do, he thought. Better to just stay with your family, make a little money, and enjoy the small pleasures of life.

Now, his dad was seventy-eight, but he had re-submerged himself deep into those years when he had a huge interest in justice. The near-deadly attack on Palmer had him fired up again. The right wing element in the military was up to its old tricks, he thought. Fascism had raised its ugly head again.

His small home in Sedalia, Missouri, located between Liberty Park and Sacred Heart High School on Third Street, was kept spick and span, except for a portion of the basement where he kept boxes of newspaper clippings, old VCR tapes and letters from United States Congressmen and Senators. All the detritus devoted to searching for clues to the deaths of the Kennedy boys and Martin Luther King.

Before he decided to send the old congressional letters to his injured son, James Morel had sat all day for a week picking through his collection: the Committee showing the Zapruder film, the negative reaction of the right-wing politicians to a request for more committee money, the resistance to subpoena power, the strength of Gonzalez to set up the investigation, the days when mob leaders Sam Giancana and Johnny Roselli disappeared.

And his blood pressure rose. "It was a coup d'etat and the right-wing did it and covered the damn thing up!"

***

Sara said, "Your dad had these sent overnight by FedEx to my pottery shop on Highway 15/501. He's trying to be careful. He's being watched, same as me. Can you imagine? FBI watching him back in Missouri? He walks down to get some smokes. FBI's watching from a parked car."

Morel nodded, "The Feds know I survived. Don't kid yourself. They could kill me any day. They want to use me in some way again. So

I think I need get outta here. You're still gonna hide me in Savannah this weekend?"

"Maybe. Too complicated just yet. You know the Deerington Village Health Center near your home? They call it the "Puke Center" because of all the hard rehab going on, sort of like the Duke Center just down the road in Fearrington Village. My workout buddy from Bally's, Andrea York, the DPT at the Center, said they've got a small workout room available for you to use. She says you can hide out there and she'll be good for your therapy, too."

"Won't that be dangerous for her, too out-in-the-open?"

"Maybe, but you'll be hidden and Andrea will visit you when she can, before work, at lunch and maybe after five pm. She's excellent. Amazing conversational style. She'll tell you stories, get you to laugh. She'll get you back in shape if anyone can. That's where you're going today. Your buddy, Coach Brad Hollofield, is taking care of the move. Tonight we gotta go."

Morel grunted. "Hollofield? Great. He's young, strong. I'll need some help to walk. Will I see Tony Jack and Cat this afternoon first, like we planned?"

Smiling, Sara said, "Of course. For a while at least."

Morel smiled, held her hand. "Thanks. What else did Dad send?"

Sara handed him the next letter from his dad. "I really can't see what these old notes are going to prove. That your dad was persistent? That these letters reveal something? Most of these people are dead or retired."

Morel saw her point, "Yes, but dad insists. He thinks I can use them somehow even now. Show that Congress was being controlled way back then. Show that the President needs to be made aware of this military control today."

Sara scoffed. "Listen. You gotta believe the President knows all of that shit. We all know. Not much he can do about it but compromise, let the military and corporations rule, keep himself alive. He's the real target now, just like JFK was, don't you think?"

"Yes. Dad's delusional, but he's right about Obama. There's no way we can help the President. He's already sold out to the corporations, not like JFK resisting the right-wing. Obama's so scared of the right-wing, he's their waterboy."

Morel thought of the politics of the 1960s assassination decade. Men who did not give up like Obama: Kennedy, King, Kennedy. The right-wing plots in cities involved in the planning of political murder:

Dallas. Memphis. Los Angeles. New Orleans. Miami. Atlanta. The South was involved in all the plots. The 1970s investigation did not get at the truth; it was merely like the old Nixonian modified, limited hang-out.

His dad's short note with the package simply said, "Check out the Georgia connection. Read Mae Brussel's theories on your computer."

Morel shrugged. He was tired of his Dad's version of the past. Not that ten-year-old kid any more, he was learning his own lessons now.

***

Brad Hollofield loved teaching and coaching. Taking time away from teaching his morning classes at North Chapel High School was not what the big, 250 pound guy wanted to do, but he had to pick up Morel at noon. Take him to the bookstore to visit his son.

Then he had the scheduled top secret journey in the early morning that would interfere with his morning classes. He'd have to take a half-day vacation. No problem. He'd take the injured Palmer Morel to Deerington Village with Sara and still get back to the school by noon.

That way he'd only miss a half-day from teaching his classes at the high school, and still get to coach football practice in the afternoon. He'd be tired but his friend Morel needed to get out of the hospital.

As a bonus, he also knew and trusted Morel's new, sexy physical therapist at Deerington Village, Andrea York, the dark-haired wild child, who hung out at the club scene in Chapel Hill, Raleigh and Durham. A real party girl by night who loved to dance, she had a definite aversion to getting too close, to allowing any men into her apartment.

One Friday he had tried, but she had smiled, touched his hand, and said, "Not tonight."

The next Friday he wanted to dance with her, but she had ignored him, turning instead to some foreign guy who could whirl and dip her as they danced in the crowded bar. Women. Brad was ready to get involved, but his best choices seemed taken or not interested.

But when Sara told him Andrea would be Morel's physical therapist, he turned happy. She was excellent, and he would also be able to visit Morel when she was there; getting a chance to talk to her might lead to something more.

His old girl, Mandy McCrae, was simply out of the picture forever. He regretted their break-up. But that was life. If Andrea would look his way, things might get good again.

But now, he had to view some film from last Friday night's game, chart some statistics on the NCHS linebackers' tackles and missed plays, and write up a report for head coach, Ed Barnes.

Barnes loved stats, loved graphs, and loved it if assistant coach Hollofield gave him percentages. Brad would write on thick cardstock with multiple color schemes, wrap them in plastic so the head coach Barnes could glance at them during practice.

Then Barnes would shout out at the team, "38 percent, 38 percent, that's what we did last week. Missed 38 percent of our tackles. Terrible. Terrible. We gotta do better against the Pittsboro Trojans on Friday. Gotta do better!"

***

During her lunch break at Deerington, Andrea went to check out the little therapy room with the single workout table. Seldom used, the room was full of supplies: bottled water, Deerington T-shirts with big bumblebees in front, extra work-out towels, stacks of computer paper.

Chomping on a tuna sandwich, she moved a few heavy boxes, dusted off the counter, retrieved a few small pillows from the cabinet and got the workout table to look more like a bed. Her visitor was a big, tall tennis player with damage to his shoulder, his back and his legs. The wounds were healing nicely, she was told, but his body was probably quite stiff, his balance no doubt a problem.

How Palmer Morel was going to sleep on such a narrow table would be problematic. Hiding out, she guessed he was desperate for any place to stay. She knew everything about him. Had to. She was tasked to help him, but also to kill him any time she got the word.

Funny, she thought. All of her training at Duke was in aiding people, improving their lives, making them stronger. But her other job was exactly the opposite. She was a trained killing machine and she had made that switch from therapist to killer frequently, twelve times in three years. From a helpful, often sexy, friend to an instant assassin with no remorse.

There were stories of women who were like black widows, setting up their husbands for death so they could collect the insurance money.

Andrea was slightly different. She set up terrorists and traitors to her country by loving them, rehabbing them, and then killing them for her country. She often wondered at her skill in treachery. Where did it come from? How could she kill with such ease, without remorse? Maybe she'd talk it over some day with her pastor or with her dad?

She laughed out loud at that idea.

Then she slid her own body onto the table. She was five foot seven and slim. Her patient was six foot two with a wide body. As she lay there looking up at the ceiling, she thought about the possibility of making love with the tennis player. Really, not enough room for two on this table. Her own arms were very close to the edge, as she lay quietly, measuring her own breathing, in-out, in-out.

Morel's dossier was full of reports of his sexual adventures over the years. The FBI had tons of women they could interview to discredit him. But the secret services wanted something else from him. What she did not know. Often a perp would be given immunity if he talked. Sometimes a new identity would be needed. Sometimes the perp could be forced into illegal acts.

Her own sexual involvement with men had frequently led to their secrets being revealed with immunity from prosecution being the bait. In those cases, it was her job to end the relationship after the secrets were recorded. She didn't miss the sex with these men. She had done her job. She wasn't involved emotionally. She argued to herself that her body was merely a tool.

Her mind wandered back to Morel and all his women. She hopped off the table, used one hand to move her long black hair behind her ear and smiled to herself. Then she extended the adjustable table-end and pictured the blond, blue-eyed tennis player stretched out nude on the narrow table, his head slightly lifted, looking at her.

What would it be like to love him? What would it be like to look deeply into his light-blue eyes? She was curious to find out.

3

The Spy at McIntyre's

Thirty-nine-year-old, sexy red-head, Cat Gallaher, and Tony Jack, Palmer Morel's spitfire son, journeyed from Deerington to McIntyre's Fine Books in the trendy retirement village of Fearrington in the early afternoon, just after lunch. A singing group called The Doozies, made up of retirees, was singing some old songs on the upper floor, and the intense fun of the old tune "Baby Face" wafted down to Cat and TJ. It seemed unusual to her singing in a bookstore, but lots of fun.

A "back-to-school" display was near the doorway, and farther inside a big stack of Paul Thompson's book, *The Terror Timeline*, hogged a space near the checkout counter. Thompson was to speak later at 2 p.m. today and the store was quickly filling with folks eager to get his book so they might gain entry to his talk to be held in The Fearrington Barn nearby.

But TJ was crazy-eager for her to read to him.

Cat made like a monkey and squatted down next to TJ as he handled the children's books on the lowest shelf, his little fingers busy turning the pages. She tried to slow him down, not wanting him to rip the pages. He loved the Richard Scarry books he had at home, *Busy, Busy Town, Cars and Trucks from A to Z*. But today he was interested in animal books: "Gimme tigers, gimme horsies, gimme sum kitty cats," he bubbled.

Playing the part of a doting mom, the ex-stripper found some cute books and tried to hide her nervousness about the meeting with Morel. Glancing out the window, she could imagine a big, dark-blue sedan parked outside, its occupants all too likely the Feds. She wanted badly to see Morel, but shaking the real Feds seemed impossible. He'd be arrested immediately, wouldn't he?

Ever since Morel had disappeared in the Haw River, the Feds questioned her repeatedly about him, on the phone, by text messages and email, often knocking on her front door until she had to open it. She had persistently told them, "He's dead, he's dead; don't you read the papers?"

But now, the latest contact from Brad assured her Morel was alive and wanted to see her. It had been arranged, Brad had said. Just spend some time with TJ, read some books at McIntyre's. And, soon, Brad would somehow get Morel to her without the Feds seeing any thing at all. Really?

She doubted that, big time. Matt and the other bookstore employees wouldn't let that happen, would they? And Phoebe, the nervous owner, was a stickler for rules.

Cat tried hard to stifle the huge catch in her throat that wanted to bring on another crying fit. She had sobbed nearly all night in disbelief and happiness, but now she felt excited and she was hyperventilating. She needed Morel to hold her, so she'd really know he was alive. But she was too paranoid to believe it would happen.

Her cell phone rang, bleating her ring tone by John Lennon, "Give Peace a Chance," cut short by a punch from her thumb.

"Yes?'

Brad's voice: "It's all set."

"Okay. Anything I can do?"

"Just stay calm, he says."

"Anything else?"

"Says he loves you."

Cat's head snapped down and she stifled an explosive sob with her hand. TJ turned to look at her with frightened toddler eyes.

Her Palmer was alive. Really. He was coming to see her. The Doozies continued their practice with an old love song: "Love and marriage, love and marriage. Go together like a horse and carriage." Cat thought she might just cry.

***

"I'd like to visit the Haw River Palmer Morel shooting site now," Colonel Max Melty gruffly told his driver as they left Chapel Hill down Hwy 15/501 in the black and silver unmarked Chrysler patrol car. After he had had a quick lunch at Mama Dip's, taking their intended path back to Raleigh.

"Yes, sir," agreed Probational Trooper Ken Niquest. "Should I notify dispatch about the change of plans?"

"Of course. We'll still be back by 1600 hours. Oh, wait a minute.

Let's stop in Fearrington Village first. McIntyre's bookstore. See if they have that new book on the Kennedy assassination."

"The book that blames the murder on organized crime only?"

"Yes. Good cover story for the real perps. Lets the New Orleans mob take most of the blame. Might be useful as a model for other projects. What's that title?"

"*Dallas Doubles.*"

"Right. Fearrington Village is just south down 15/501 before we get to the river."

"Yes, sir. I know. My grandparents live there in one of the condos on Langdon."

"A good quiet place. Lots of trees. Nice old people."

Niquest agreed, "Not like Deerington, that's for sure."

Melty thought for a moment, "You know. I fought against that damn Deerington Village. All those friggin' neon lights. Those bees whirling about. The drugs. The parties. I'd love to close that place down."

Choosing his words carefully, Niquest replied, "I'm sure many people feel that way. But, you know, I live there. I love it. Great young families. Lots of play areas for kids and a real community feeling. And by the way, I checked for drugs before I moved in. None at all. I think there's lots more drugs, legal and illegal, in Fearrington with those old people from the crazy 1960s running around……."

Melty interrupted, "Are you fuckin' crazy? Why'd you move there? You want to jeopardize your probationary status? Jesus, I just don't understand. You seem damned conservative. How could you move into some kinda psychedelic rat hole like Deerington?"

***

Morel hated hospitals. Hated the food. Hated the nights in the uncomfortable hospital bed. Hated peeing in a cup. But today was the worst day yet.

Promised a quick release at noon, he was out of patience now, only Sara's own quiet and calm demeanor keeping him halfway positive.

"Look. It's been a half hour. I'm waiting. I'm dressed. Hollofield's probably in the parking lot. Shit! Get me outta here."

Sara said, "Palmer. I agree with you. It's nerve-racking. But, really, the paper work is almost done. One more person has to check off on it."

"I know. I know. The same friggin' nurse that never answered the buzzer when I needed help. Where is she?"

"Listen. The nurse's desk can't find her either. I suggested they look outside. She likes her smokes, you know."

Morel ranted, "What's a nurse smoking for? It's a hospital. She's a nurse. And she smokes? What the fuck."

Sara left the room, quickly returning. "She's coming now, Palmer."

Then the nurse rolled a wheelchair through the door. "We're ready," she announced. "I wasn't smoking Mr. Morel." She gave him a look.

Sara helped Morel off the bed. He took a few tentative steps to the wheelchair and sat down. The nurse adjusted the footrest, got the wheelchair turned around, smacking Morel's foot against the table.

Morel took a deep breath in pain, but said nothing. Soon they were scooting over to the elevator with Sara following behind, a big smile on her face. "The nurse told me Hollofield's downstairs," she said.

***

Niquest stayed with the car parked outside The Belted Goat restaurant as Melty hopped out, going across the green divider in the little Village of Fearrington to McIntyre's Books.

"*Dallas Doubles, Dallas Doubles,*" Melty repeated to himself, looking both ways then crossing the street. *Sounds like a tennis book or something faggish like that,* he grumbled.

He loved the smell of McIntyre's, all those books, plus the added pleasure of a perfumed Susan, his favorite non-fiction expert for the bookstore. Inside the store he looked to his right. No Susan. He walked left to the book counter. "Susan workin' today?" he asked the pudgy clerk.

Matt answered, "Sir?"

"Susan workin' today?"

"Yes, she's in back. Can I help you?"

"No, not you. Get Susan. She knows what's she's doin'."

Matt turned and walked through the doorway. Melty could hear him talking. Someone said, "Oh, no." Then, Matt returned to the counter.

"Susan's quite busy now. May I help?" Matt asked again.

Melty was provoked. "Just tell her Max Melty's here. She'll understand. I don't need you."

Matt disappeared again and Melty sized up the store. Two customers in the kids' section. A stack of books by that pinko writer Thompson, about the 9/11 terror attack, a few ladies whispering over by fiction.

A shuffle or a commotion began to filter into his consciousness. Turning away from the books, Melty listened hard. The back door down a corridor was open, letting in some warmer air, and voices were whispering, something moving, rolling along. So, he moved away from the back door and waited, picked up the hated book, *Terror Timeline*, pretending to read.

***

With Sara Jensen leading the way, Hollofield moved the wheelchair along the narrow entryway, Morel keeping his arms tucked in, his heart rate increasing, a big smile on his face. His son and favorite girl were waiting for him somewhere near the kids' books section. Sara moved herself a few steps out of the way, giving Hollofield a clear shot with the wheelchair straight toward the kids' books.

A quick turn past the pile of red-covered *Terror Timelines* and Morel could see TJ on the floor with Cat beside him, their backs turned, engrossed in some big picture book. Morel gave out a huge train *TOOT*, one he was sure TJ would respond to immediately since he had used it nearly every day at home when he needed TJ to come running.

Hollofield was stunned by the shrill noise and stopped abruptly, Morel holding on so he didn't fall off. The rest of the bookstore reacted too, everyone stock still, their faces turned to Morel, their mouths open, one older lady holding her ears. Morel gave another, "*TOOT*."

TJ hopped up, his little feet scooting along the floor, turning past displays of books until he ran into the wheelchair and jumped on his dad's lap. "I see daddy." the little kid hollered.

Everyone smiled except Melty.

***

Matt rang up the sale of the assassination book, *Dallas Doubles,* and handed the debit card back to Melty. But Melty wasn't looking. He was observing the tender scene in the front room of the bookstore. The crippled man was hugging a gorgeous redhead who was kneeling beside his wheelchair, while an Asian woman held hands with a little boy of about two who was hooting like a long train going up hill. Other spectators watched the scene developing close by, the Fearrington women's book club fawned with delight, and a few old men stood nearby dressed in "The Doozies: We Crank You Up!" T-shirts and carrying song books. Soon they were singing an old song called "Baby Face" and most of the crowd joined in.

Matt tapped Melty's shoulder and he finally collected his debit card and a paper bag containing his purchase. "God Dammit," he whispered as he made his way out the front door and over the grassy divider to his waiting car.

Niquest reached over and opened the door. Melty was getting worse, his anger causing him to sputter. "Get Tandy and Milstrum, get the fuckin' Siler City crew. Have 'em set up outside the bookstore now, no sirens, nothin' but speed. Tell 'em we got that traitor Palmer Morel.

Tell 'em to set up a perimeter too, out on 15/501."

***

The Doozies wrapped up their singing and gingerly walked toward the front door. The eldest member, Dick Nimmick, held the door open, and stood a bit perplexed soon after.

A stocky gentleman was running across the parking lot, heading for some sort of police car, no markings, some other guy in the driver's seat.

Dick grumbled, "Friggin' coppers," and then wodered what was going on. Lots of animated talk and pointing toward the book store.

But then the glint from the sun hit Dick's eyeglasses, his eyes burned white light and he got confused. He fought the confusion, tried to sit down on the steps outside the book store, missed, and bumped onto the pavement instead, holding onto the branch from a small tree.

Most of the Doozies had already gone to their own cars, but Dick's legs lay in the cool shade of the grass, his head down on the hot pavement, his glasses tossed lightly onto a bed of pine straw.

Sara watched the group leave and thought the old dudes were

cute. She left Palmer hugging his girl friend and kid, crossed over to the window and saw the Doozie Dick on the pavement.

"Brad! Brad!" she called over to Hollofield. "Some old man fell down outside. He's hurt. Call 911."

4

Escape from McIntyre's

"What the shit!" Max Melty said. His driver, Trooper Niquest, sat still. Best to just listen.

The police radio was squawking. "Man down in Fearrington Village outside McIntyre's Books. Rescue 21, Pumper 34, enroute at twelve-forty-seven."

Melty listened, too. He could hear sirens now, coming from the volunteer fire department right across the highway. "What the fuck? Where's the Patrol?"

Niquest said, "Forming a perimeter. Tandy's group has deployed near the barn. You can see 'em over there, by the gate."

Melty looked, "Okay, okay. Nothing messed up too bad. Get me Tandy."

Niquest used his radio. "Officer Tandy? Here's Colonel Melty."

"We got a glitch, Tandy," Melty spoke to Tandy. "What's your 20? By the barn? Okay. Some old guy fell down out front. Give the ambulance time to get over here and leave. Watch all doors of the book store. Morel's inside. We got him trapped. Big blond guy in a wheelchair. Can't miss him."

Tandy was brief, "10—4."

***

"You gotta say goodbye," Hollofield urged Morel. "I see a patrol car outside."

"How do you know?" asked Cat Gallaher. "For god's sake, we just got here. TJ needs his dad."

Morel pulled her head down to his wheelchair. "Hollofield knows. We gotta go. I'll call soon. Here's a big hug."

Cat and TJ stood very still as Hollofield pushed Morel to the doorway. However, a big white/green ambulance was backing up the front path to the book store. Matt and Susan from the store were helping position the ambulance in place. Two EMT's jumped out and went to the old man on the ground.

"Morel. You gotta go with the ambulance," whispered Hollofield.

"What the hell?' asked Morel.

"You gotta go with the hurt old guy. Those are my buddies in the ambulance, them two EMT's. I'll talk to 'em. They'll take you to the Deerington Center after they drop off the old guy at the hospital."

Morel started to object, but Hollofield picked him out of the wheelchair, put him over his shoulder and hopped down the outside steps to the back of the ambulance, climbing inside and dumping Morel down next to the stretcher. "Stay here. I'll tell my EMT friends. You keep your head down. Remember: see Andrea at the Center."

Morel watched as the EMT's loaded the hurt Doozie singer inside, placing the guy's glasses in a plastic bag on the front of his blue Doozies T-shirt.

In the background, he caught a glimpse of Cat and TJ, and then watched Hollofield in the doorway as he put himsef into the wheelchair. *Goddam. Hollolfield's gonna take my place*, he thought.

The ambulance door slammed shut, the siren went on, Morel wobbled a bit, then he was on his was out of Fearrington Village.

***

Near 1 p.m. outside the window, Andrea spotted an ambulance enter the circle drive at the Deerington Center. Green and white, this emergency vehicle or others like it often visited the exercise area, awakening young guys who fainted, helping oldsters with confusion after too much time on the Stepper, taking vital signs on a few swimmers who were semi-conscious but soon fully awake.

But this visit was odd. Two EMT's half-carrying someone from the ambulance surreptitiously through the back door: a big guy with blond hair, not able to walk too well. Was this her new, secret patient, Mr. Palmer Morel, tennis pro, womanizer, terrorist?

Crazy! Much too early for Morel to be here. Something bad must have happened. The schedule was completely off. Arriving in daytime? There seemed to be no way for her to hide him now. That is, unless she could rush to her office, grab that fright wig from the last big party over at Duke, cover him with a sheet and then stuff him in the little room she had prepared under the steps. All without being seen.

It was just after lunchtime, only a couple of members, otherwise how to explain this caper to Ms Oakwood her supervisor or anyone else? A good story might be Morel didn't want to be seen exercising? He was a recluse? He wanted his privacy? He was simply odd. But how could she sign him in? She hadn't made out his pass card. He hadn't paid anything on account. He was not a member. Ms Oakwood would know.

She jogged to the room under the stairs, opened the door, moved boxes out of the way. Then, she slid the Center's wheelchair from behind the front counter, pushed it past the few members on the stationary bikes in front of the TV sets and met the EMT's as they came inside.

Morel slumped onto the wheelchair and Andrea pushed the wig on his head, flopped a sheet over his body and told him to shut up.

The EMT's smiled. They thought they knew what was happening. Hollofield had told them Morel was avoiding his ex-wife. They believed that and walked away chuckling. Anything to help friends in their traumatic, marital needs.

"This is your home for a while, Mr. Morel. So, I'm your new therapist, Dr. Andrea York." She shook his hand. Morel gave his bright smile, his blue eyes looking her up and down.

"You'll do," he joked. "When's lunch?"

Andrea straightened his wig. "Lunch? So, I'm your therapist, not some waitress. Now let me show you to your new room."

Morel shrugged. "Do I have a choice?"

***

No options with the police, so TJ and Cat answered questions. They sat in the back room of McIntyre's Books. Cat should call a lawyer but she didn't. Max Melty hovered nearby, his video machine grinding away, recording nothing of interest.

"I know nothing," Cat repeated. "I was told to be here at noon. I came at noon. I got to see my friend Palmer Morel for a few minutes. All hell broke loose. Here I am with you."

"Where'd he go? Who helped him get out of here.?"

"As I told you. His friend Brad Hollofield was contacted to bring him to the book store. He did. TJ and I waited. They came in. I gave Morel a hug. All hell broke loose."

Melty gave it another twist. "Do you have your cell phone?"

"No."

"Do you own a cell phone.?"

"Yes."

"Okay. Did you receive a message on your cell to be here?"

"Maybe."

Melty told Niquest, "Make a note. Get a search warrant for Cat Gallaher's home with access to her phone records."

***

Morel signed a few papers Andrea York put in front of him, as a cover for his treatment at the Deerington Center. Fake name. Fake unsurance policy. Fake doctor's orders. All compliments to the ingenuity of a well-trained physical therapy graduate trained to fill out Medicare forms and use insurance-speak.

Andrea explained, "These will do for now. So, I'm using the forms for another patient who's on a trip to Europe now. But at some point, I'll have to get you out of here. So then, my other patient might notice something on his bill or my supervisor might get a phone call for authorization or something. Anyway, I agreed to help you. So, Sara's my friend. But you might have to move again, quickly. You can do it, right? You're a tennis pro."

Morel said, "Yes, I play. Do you?"

Andrea joked, "Yes, I do too. And I bet I can beat your butt now in your pathetic condition."

Morel laughed out loud. "I don't think so. I'll run you around until you beg for mercy. I'll challenge you when I get better."

It was Andrea's time to smile. "Listen, Mr. Morel. I'm your doctor, not your tennis partner. But, maybe. Maybe I'll play later."

There was a short pause, Morel thinking. "So, what's my new name?"

"Stephen Milgram. You're an insurance adjustor for All State in Chapel Hill."

"Hmm. Sales. Don't like it, but okay. But, listen. I'm hungry. When do I eat?"

"I get off work at 5 pm. And then, I'll go home. It will get dark. The Center closes at 10 pm. And then, I'll get back here at 10:30 with some food. So, stay in this room. And do these leg and arm exercises from this sheet. Stay limber. Part of your therapy, no? Here, you can use my extra cell phone for entertainment. So, I've got games on there, music, the internet, so keep the volume way down. And don't call anyone, except me if you're in trouble or something. See, my number's on the address book. See, look here for Andi. That's my name. And stay cool. There's some bottled water on that shelf."

"Andi, that's seven hours I've got to wait?"

"Be patient, so I'm locking the door now. Be good….so, if you have to pee, I've got a big, empty plastic water jug over in the corner."

"Should I keep taking my meds?"

"Sure. What do you have?"

"Iron, stool softener, vitamins, oxycontin."

"Well, don't take the oxycontin any more. Shouldn't you be off it by now?"

"I guess. I just use it for pain once in awhile."

"Geez, maybe we'll get you off it starting right now. You got any side effects from the drug?"

"No. Just some strange dreams. I've been writing them down. Weird. Funny."

"Listen to me. Those dreams really are a side effect. They are. So, stay cool. Stay off the pain killer. See you soon."

Morel watched her jog to the door, close it, and disappear, her quick, light, athletic steps fading away. Morel was intrigued.

***

Finally relaxing, Morel played with Andrea's old iPhone, checking the local news, watching a few news videos with the volume way low, a special report on an incident in Fearrington Village.

A reporter from WRAL was standing outside McIntyre's Books, speaking in that odd newscaster staccato voice, a phony voice always with too much punch. Morel wondered if all these news clones went to the same media school.

"Police are refusing to answer ANY questions about the escape of a wanted man here in Fearrington. Colonel Melty of the highway patrol issued a SHORT statement, but walked away WITHOUT answering reporters' question. Back to you, Cynthia."

The video accompanying the report showed the same scene over and over. It was Brad Hollofield being led away to a squad car. Then a close-up of Cat looking sad, a tear washing down her cheek. Then a quick shot of TJ, holding Cat's hand and looking forlorn.

Morel clicked off the phone, then slowly leaned back on his new, narrow bed. "Shit, shit, shit," was all he could say. He'd love to call Cat, but that was forbidden.

***

Sleep came to Morel fast. He sighed a few times, turned over on his side carefully, tucked a pillow under his arm and was completely zonked in about a minute.

But the oxycontin effects kicked in too, and soon he plunged into a computerized nightmare, a dream connected to his situation, to Andrea and her iPhone, and to the tennis challege he had issued to her.

Weird, waking up then, he tried messaging Andrea on FACEBOOK, searching for her name until he found it on-line, available to all. He buzzed through some of her old photos: laughing at the camera, giving some sort of wide-open mouth grimace, full of fun, dancing like crazy at some party, a drink in her hand. Then, he messaged her:

"Andi. I just had a lovely game of make-believe tennis with you during my crazy oxicontin afternoon nightmare, but you were beastly, absolutely beastly, to me, in the dream. You hit well in practice, very consistent, your pale green tennis dress flapping, your yellow top and bright white tennis visor flashing in the sun.

But, then, we started, and you knew, just knew, about my bad kness. From side to side you ran me, once in awhile hitting a lob down the middle to let me catch my breath, I guess. Then, you'd bring me to the net with a drop shot, lob one over my head winning the point, then laughing uproariously at me.

I won a few of my serves, but you won the first set 6--3, then you were leading 3--1 when you broke off, sipping on some cool lemonade in a cooler you shared with me. Sorry, you said. I must leave. I've got to go home, shower then meet a friend for a beer at Brixx. Maybe we can play again if you're not too intimidated? You laughed again, sprinted to your car and zoomed off.

I limped to a bench in the shade behind the court, looked up into the leaves of a big tree, and regained my poise. I'll get her next time, I vowed. Then I looked for the Dunlop tennis balls. They were gone. You had taken the cooler and the tennis balls with you. Damn!"

"Great nightmare, huh?" he texted. He didn't wait long.

Andrea answered quickly, "Cute dream:)"

***

Morel's disappearance had left a gap at the Deerington Tennis Club. His tennis office had stayed untouched except for the black crepe around the doorway and his smiling photo tacked on the cork board nearby.

His evening ladies group had attached a formal note card and individual members scrawled their grief in sometimes poetic format, remembering Morel's wit and corny jokes.

"We'll never forget you, Palm."

"Don't worry. We still hustle."

"Stay focused, Palm."

"Now you've really graduated, Summa Cum Piña Colada." Only married-to-the-mob Mrs. Dolores "Dolly" Minori kept her distance, still practicing her tennis but avoiding any memories of Morel. She hated the thought of that bastard and wished he rotted in hell.

Upset with the club manager, Morris Decker, she had told him to take down the little Morel memorial, but Decker resisted.

This afternoon, Dolly was using the ball machine, practicing her very weak backhand and dressed in her favorite yellow, low-cut tennis dress. She did look sort of cute out there on court four, grunting with every shot like Sharapova, moving those once-glamorous chunky legs and using the f-word any time she missed a shot. Young mothers made a detour around her court, pushing their kids away from her bad language and cleavage.

Dolly had a theory fed by mob rumors about Morel's death: he wasn't dead at all. One of the dancers at her husband's Durham strip club had supposedly visited the hospital for an infected blister on her foot. During her overnight stay, she was placed on Floor Seven, the orthopedic operation floor. In the hallway, a tall man was practicing walking with his crutches.

Accompanied by a younger Asian woman, the man had looked into her room and she saw his piercing blue eyes staring into hers. She recognized him instantly. Palmer Morel had visited the strip club many times. A good tipper, he had made many friends; some girls had even played on his summer softball team in Pittsboro.

Dolly needed to call the hospital after her practice session. She needed to see if she could visit Morel, if he was still there. She needed proof he was still alive.

5

Detention

"Wake up, Palmer. Wake up." It was 10:30 pm and Morel was sleeping deeply, one leg sprawled off the little workout table at the Deerington Center. Finally, his blue eyes opened.

"Andi? What? Time to eat?"

Andrea York was serious now, very serious. Her orders had come from Fort Bragg. She was ready to move.

"Palmer. I know you've had a tough day cooped up here, but we have to get out of here now. The TV news is showing your photo. Your friend Hollofield has been questioned by police. He gave you up. So, now everyone in North Carolina knows you're alive. So, you can't stay here any more."

Sitting upright now, Morel shook off the blanket. His entire body glowed nude in the dark. Andrea did not avert her eyes. *God, he's beautiful*, she thought.

"Do you feel okay? Are you stiff? So, can I get you out of here now?"

He slipped off the table and stood in front of her, flexing his back, his arms, lifting his legs one by one. "I can go, if you say so. Are they looking for me?"

She watched him carefully, her physical therapy expertise judging his body. He had great strength. He would respond well to her therapy. "Not yet, but Sara called and she's very worried. She thinks they'll try to take your life. You know, shoot first, ask questions later."

She reached out her right hand and moved it across his back, his scarred chest and down past his groin to his knees. She squatted down to get a better look at his legs, holding one of them with her strong hands, then the other, having him lift his leg, setting his leg down.

Moving her arms, she turned him around. She traced the bullet wound in his back above his buttocks, feeling the wound's rough edges. She reached into the cabinet and brought out some lotion. She squirted a bit on the wound, rubbing the liquid softly into his skin.

She paused, breathing deeply. "Maybe you'd better get dressed. You seem strong enough to make a long trip tonight."

She stood up, tried to touch his chest wound, wrapped her arms around his chest, began to trace the scar from his groin up to his chest, but softly grazed his genitals by mistake. Noticing his reaction, she concluded he was certainly ready for anything.

She changed her plan slightly. "I think we have a little time for your first therapy session. At least a half hour. Please lie back down on the table."

As Morel slowly lay down, she squirted the lotion generously on his muscular thighs, rubbed it in softly and then took all the time she needed to get him relaxed.

She slipped out of her top, removed her bra, and laid her head on his chest, reached her bare arm onto his belly, and moved her strong fingers, squeezing, squeezing until she felt him shudder.

She looked deeply into his blue eyes. She knew then she could never follow an order to kill him.

He sighed, "Where are you taking me?"

She answered, "To Heaven. We're going to Savannah."

***

At the tennis club, it was late and Dolly Minori finished her shower, using some body lotion on her aging knees and thighs. She could hear the racquet club manager talking just outside the locker room. The junior girls had finished their "tough tennis" routine, and Morris Decker was chatting them up. Obviously, he liked these teenage girls.

Dolly closed up the lotion, put it in her gym bag, and then laced up her shoes. Her hair was still a bit wet from the shower, but she wanted to confront Decker.

Walking out of the locker room, she spotted him strolling away toward the steps leading to the courts. His arm was around "Bipper" Butterfield's shoulder, and the sixteen-year-old was leaning toward him, picking up some advice.

Bip, named for the sound her racquet made when she was just a little girl, was the club's noted advertisement, often seen on WRAL-TV whacking away at center court and then talking into the camera, praising the professional staff at Deerington, notably Palmer Morel when he was still "alive" and not a terrorist. Dolly thought she was disgustingly blonde and gorgeous, flaunting her breasts in her bouncy, low-cut blouse. Dolly heard that membership figures had grown huge after just two weeks after that Bipper ad.

She called out, "Decker, Decker, come back here."

The gray-haired tennis pro stopped, took his right arm off Bip's body and turned. "Yes, Mrs. Minori?"

He said a quick goodbye to Bip, and then used his left hand to pat her little behind as she left for her ride home.

"You'll get in trouble for that some day," said Dolly.

Decker just smiled.

"You're just like that womanizer Palmer Morel, you know. Say, a friend of mine was over at the UNC hospital. She says she saw Morel over there in a hallway. And he's alive isn't

he? Decker, you hear me? Morel's alive, isn't he?"

Decker wasn't smiling, running his fingers through his steel-gray hair, but he said, "Yes."

Dolly grunted. "I need to go see him tonight. I want you to drive me."

"Dolly, you're too late. Didn't you see the news? He's not at the hospital. The police are after him. He's escaped."

***

The little car sped past the old soda shoppe, the S&T, past Virlie's Restaurant and sped west off the traffic circle toward the community college, stopping a block away from the detention center on West Street in Pittsboro. Andrea parked her red Kia and fussed with a manila folder, removing an even smaller envelope.

Morel was stretched out on the back seat of the little car, one seat belt around his waist, the phony, floppy fright-wig hanging half off his head.

"What's up, Andi?"

"I'm going inside. Maybe they'll let me speak to Brad."

"You want me to wait here? What if you don't come back? What if they hold you for questioning or something?"

"Listen," she told Morel through the open driver's side window. "They don't know me, but if I don't come back in fifteen minutes, get out of here. The keys are in the ignition. Drive yourself down south on 95 to Bonaventure Cemetery like we planned. Sara will be there to meet you."

She took off briskly, staying in the shadows, walking past the parked sheriff vehicles, then in through the side door toward the admittance desk. She knew all the guys here that worked days; this night crew was new to her but her ID would get her to the cell block she was sure.

"Evening. I'm here to see Brad Hollofield," she announced.

The bulky but buff officer looked up from his paper work, frowned and stood up, approaching the visitor. "Hollofield's not seeing anyone tonight, Miss. You're not his lawyer, are you? You some journalist?"

Andrea leaned on the tall reception desk. "No, I'm not. I'm US Army. Fort Bragg. I have military ID." She pulled out her card and pushed it toward the officer.

"Okay. Hmmm. Special Ops. Birth 8-1-81. This picture looks younger. Let your hair grow did you?"

"Yes, sir. New assignment now."

"Okay. But I need two ID's."

"Yes, sir. Will this do?" She offered her other Bragg ID, her entrance badge, a RAPIDGate Badge that let her into Fort Bragg without hassle.

"Okay. Reason for entrance to the cell at this late hour?"

"Interrogation. Subject Hollofield might have ties to Fort Bragg."

"He's sleeping. He's not talking. His lawyer says no visitors."

"I'm not a visitor. He'll talk to me. Wake him up."

The officer took her card and swiped it into his computer. He was denied access. "I can't get your information from Fort Bragg."

"Special Ops, sir. No access for anyone without override."

"Well, Sergeant Andrea York, then I can't get you access to the cell block either. Come back in the morning with specific paperwork."

"Officer, I need to talk to Hollofield now. Maybe this ID will help?" She pulled out the small brown envelope from the car. As he reached for it, she shoved one long hairpin through his index finger and into his hand. The liquid's effect was immediate and painful.

The officer fell hard onto the tiled floor.

"So sorry, sir. You were in the way," Andrea muttered.

***

After the long search of her condo in Deerington Village, Cat Gallaher was exhausted. She sat in the sun room, looking out on the deck, the night noises of insects rising up loudly.

Five officers, four hours, and they only thing they took was her cell phone. "You might have contacts we are interested in," was the only reason given. Lucky she had her new iPhone in the car.

Of course, that's why she had waved the right to a search warrant. She and Morel had nothing to hide. No documents, no contraband, no betting slips, no gambling paraphernalia. Nothing. They weren't secret agents, terrorists or dangerous to anyone. It was all bullshit stirred up by some fanatic right-wing neighbor.

She thought of the visit with Morel at McIntyre's Books, so disappointing: one hug, a smile and then he was gone. Little TJ was a wreck too. He needed his dad and just seeing him got him so excited. Then, the abrupt departure and the whole separation anxiety thing came back: poor TJ, the wailing, the deep sadness. Before he got to sleep in his little jammies, he wandered all over the condo asking, "Dad, dad, daddy?" The little kid was heart-broken again. And so was Cat.

She reached for the TV remote, clicked it on. There was the photo of her Palmer for all the word to hate. *Call 555-TIPS if you have any information.*

"Information?" Cat bellowed at the TV. "Why don't you give me the information on why you want Palmer dead?"

***

At 6'4" and 250 pounds, Hollofield was much too big for his cell, something like a 7' by 10' birdcage, the bed much too narrow, the window looking out at a bright yellow streetlight much too tiny. Hearing someone coming down the hall, he got up, grabbed the bars, and looked through like some big, white gorilla at the zoo.

Andrea gave him the quiet sign, one finger on her lips, her body hurrying down the shiny corridor to him. She was good at her job.

But what was her job? Hollofield didn't know. He watched as she pulled out a hand-sized piece of metal from her pocket and placed it over the lock at the door. Was it a magnet? She pushed a few buttons on the lock in a random manner and his cell popped open.

Still giving him the "hush" gesture, she grabbed his hand and pulled him out to the main desk, then down another corridor toward the side door. Hollofield was astounded to see the detention officer lying on the tile floor, completely unconscious.

Outside, they took off running. "We got you. We got you," Andrea was saying.

Hollofield wondered, *Yeah, but what now?*

***

Max Melty did not like interference from outside law enforcement, and he chafed when he was forced to talk by phone with a Fort Bragg contact. Yes, Morel's buddy Hollofield had escaped from the Pittsboro detention center, but he could handle that and find Morel, too.

What the fuck did the Army know about catching criminals?

Finding Morel alive was a bit of luck, but Melty wanted to control this capture operation. He could summon the help of the highway patrol all across the state and get aid from neighboring states as well.

Shit, what could the Army do, call out the troops? No way. They had messed up the Morel affair at the Haw River. They had the chance to kill Morel and failed. He angrily picked up the phone in his office.

"This is Melty."

"Let it go, Max. We're handling it."

"Then you must know something I don't."

"Just let it go. We've got inside contacts."

Melty steamed, "We're the ones got burned. People want answers. Results."

"Never mind. This is national security. We got it covered."

"So, you're tellin' me to do nothin'?"

"That's right."

"But we got a mysterious death here, at the detention center."

"We know. Say you're waiting for the autopsy. Tell the news that the Feds are launching an investigation, a manhunt."

Melty groaned, "But here we don't really get to do a thing."

"That is correct. We'll handle it."

6

Bonaventure

A quick call to Sara and Morel had set the time to meet her in Charleston. She was already scooting down 95 before they got off the 40 interchange to 95.

She said she had called a friend at The Citadel, a part-time art teacher, a Savannah State grad, gay, but he had a convertible couch in his sun room, at his apartment in North Charleston. Easy access off 26 highway on Sabal Street. No problem.

Hollofield has happy to be free, but worried. No football coaching job now. No future. Nothing but Andrea and she seemed attracted to Morel.

"You okay, Brad?" Andrea asked from her front seat.

"Not really."

"We can get you down to Savannah later."

"Yeah?"

"Sure. We got Palmer a place there. We'll work on uniting with you soon. Scott's a nice guy. You'll like him."

"Sara said he's gay."

"Yes, but Sara says he's very reliable. Has a friend, a partner. Not a sleep-in but close. You know how gays operate, right?"

"Not really. And, Andrea, you killed that guy, right, at the jail? You killed him."

Andrea didn't answer.

"You killed him, so I'm an accessory to murder or something, something more serious than helping Palmer escape. I'm right, aren't I? I'm correct? Right? Right?"

Andrea sighed, "It had to be done."

***

He looked like an artist, a gay artist, thin, splattered jeans, dirty white T-shirt, bare feet, longish blond hair, one discreet tattoo on his upper left arm. Scott invited Sara inside, gave her a hug.

It was after midnight but he offered her some wine. Sara declined, parked herself in the kitchen. Took a bottled water instead.

"He's a nice guy, big like I told you. Football's his game, not art. A high school coach."

"But he's in trouble, you said. Big trouble. Has to hide out."

"Yeah, I know. It's a big favor but he won't be here long. Just a few days. I'm taking him to Savannah. I'll give you a call."

Scott looked at his watch. "I've got an eight o'clock. Gotta get some sleep."

"He'll be here. He's driving right behind me. Don't worry."

"Is the guy gonna be hungry? Should I make some sandwiches?"

"His name's Brad. Yeah. He can probably eat. He's a huge guy, and…"

The bell rang. "Buzz him up, Scott. That'll be him."

Scott walked to the door, hit the buzzer, and he could hear heavy steps marching up to the second floor.

Sara looked out the back window toward the parking lot. A small red car was already leaving.

Scott opened the door.

"Hi, Brad," said Sara. "Gotta go now."

Brad stood there a moment, shrugged and walked into a gay man's apartment for the first time ever.

***

Leaving Scott's apartment, Sara pulled her Karmann Ghia behind Andrea's Kia, getting onto 26 and going toward 95. It would take maybe an hour to get to Savannah, and then they'd go to Bonaventure Cemetery and find the old Henry Mitchell crypt Sara had used during her college days two years ago.

    Sara found that Henry Mitchell had been some local Savannah dude during the turn of the 19th century, owned a consulting business for foreign trade, kept track of ships in the harbor, introduced foreign businessmen to the locals, sponsored many gorgeous parties in the now historic part of Savannah just off Abercorn.

    When he died, his spacious crypt was built in Section L, near Stoddard Way. Over the years, visitors, weather and vandals had damaged the front door just enough that Sara and her clever artist friends were able to use the space inside the crypt for quiet beer parties and for a few sexual escapades. After their adventures, they used a creative wrought iron clasp to keep the door shut and secure-looking. The Mitchell crypt was the place Sara had chosen for Morel's temporary hideaway.

    As the two cars moved down Bay Street in Savannah, Sara phoned Andrea. "Pull over and wait for me. I'll go ahead of you and you can follow over to Bonaventure."

    "Okay, but Palmer's hungry. Should we grab a bite?"

Sara wondered, "Not sure if anything's open now, anything quick anyway. Maybe just get some sleep for now and eat in the morning. It's 3 am, you know?"

Sara pulled ahead of Andrea and took the Truman Parkway south to Victory Drive. A few more blocks and she was on Bonaventure Road, the dark, curvy drive to the Cemetery.

"We're here," Sara announced, parking her car toward the north side of the cemetery. Andrea pulled behind, dousing her lights.

"C'mon," said Sara. "Follow me around the fence and east toward the bluff." She slogged along in the dark, with Morel and Andrea trying to keep up in the blackness, no moon out tonight.

***

Chilly, the breeze coming to Bonaventure Cemetery from the east, off the ocean, Palmer Morel pulled on the elastic of his black sweatpants with his right hand, trying to cover his stomach, giving up on his floppy green hoodie which he had used as a pillow. It lay somewhere behind him in the Mitchell crypt.

Autumn brought mostly beautiful thoughts of his childhood years and a warm bed, but this morning was awkward once and cold. Andi seemed lost. She went out at 7 am to get some food, but where was she?

It was now almost 8 am. He was really hungry. He reached for her old iPhone.

He texted her quickly: *Andi. I'm awake. I'm hungry. Where are you?*

He thought all these stupid precautions unnecessary now. Three weeks had gone by, his health was better, and his appetite definitely back to normal.

He rolled slowly unto his left side, the side uninjured by bullets or smashed by the roiling of massive tree trunks in the Haw River. Of course, he knew he was lucky. Of course, he owed his life to Sara his lovely artist and to his burly fireman friend, Brad Hollofield.

But even injured as he was, he was able to win the heart of a new girl with auburn hair. His 5'8" physical therapist who gives great massages, his sexy friend. He feels he's learned almost everything about her.

He knows Andi's thirty, but she seems younger. She just got out of a bad relationship, and loves dancing, beer and pizza. This proud, professional woman even walked out on her therapist job in Deerington Village to take him to Savannah. Hard to believe she did that for him.

***

Andrea loved the old seventies tunes, and now they had special meaning for her. Todd Rundgren was singing "I Saw the Light" as she sped her little red Kia around the curves on Bonaventure on her way to the Piggly Wiggly over on Victory near Skidaway. Yes, she had seen some kind of light in Morel's eyes, but this light promised more personal involvement than she wanted.

Andrea knew that Morel was trouble. The 6' 2" blond couldn't be hidden easily, but Sara using her contacts at Savannah State had somehow found a place for him at Bonaventure Cemetery in a beautiful old crypt. That seemed okay for a few days, but Andrea's instincts vibrated. Morel could never stay cooped up there for a week ot even a day.

And leaving her job in Deerington Village had been crazy. Where would Fort Bragg be able to get her a PT job now? On some mid-eastern battlefield? Besides, how could she stay here with him when Cat, his old girl, and Sara, his newest girl, might want access to him? Is she supposed to step outside the crypt when he fucks them? This was crazy, crazy love twist.

She hesitated a moment in the Piggly Wiggly when he texted her. He's hungry, he says. She's been gone too long. Shit! It's been only half an hour and he's already going crazy in the crypt.

Now what could she buy that wouldn't spoil quickly out at Bonaventure?

7

The Plum Puddin'

Canned goods and potato chips. Single soups and two-sided peanut butter crackers. Bottled water and cashews. Most of it seemed healthy and Andi put it in her backseat.

She checked the car both inside and out but couldn't find any little gadgets from the Feds..

She knew someone had stashed a GPS on board. Common sense. And if she found it, she wouldn't take it off. A simple procedure. And actually she felt safer knowing Bragg was doing its job, checking her safety. But she would like to find it.

Frustrated and wasting time, she also needed to stop at the local flea market. She needed some new threads to match her new look. She had purchased hair coloring, scissors and applicators.

She needed a makeover, maybe new color hair, new clothes, new job, even if she was hiding in plain sight. Morel liked her normal take-charge demeanor, thinking she was hiding out like he was. It would be her little secret. Hiding out from no one.

But there was no doubt the mob, doing the FBI's bidding, had traced Morel to the Triangle and then followed him to Savannah. Why not? It was their job to scapegoat Morel at some point in time. Maybe as someone to blame again for some mob hit.

Could she help keep Palmer Morel safe? She would if necessary. She admitted she couldn't kill him now, and she was bonded to him, but how could she stop anyone else?

Rows and rows of useless clothing inside the Pecan Pie Store. Andrea wanted to adopt the tight-jean look with a bedazzler top, and would cut her black hair and add some purplish or magenta streaks. She'd still use her shortened name, Andi, and still be hot, but not the calm, athletic type any more. It worked on Palmer and attracted other men which caused her some concern.

Her new look would be edgier, scare away the unwanted, and she could use her entire battalion of swear words on Morel. Shake him up. Tell him it's good therapy. Andi liked portraying the tough girl. Got her through special ops training. She'd show Morel she could be very aggressive now, while being protective of him at the same time.

Returning to her car with some tough new duds, she smiled when she thought of Morel's reaction to her new persona.

***

Morel grew more impatient, but a few text messages kept him amused. Sara was back in Chapel Hill, her pottery shop lively already this morning. "Crazy busy. No cop problems. Got three pots sold already. Still having my toast and coffee. Five cars in the lot. All Pittsboro citizens. Guess the spies aren't watching me any more."

Morel wrote back: "All good. Thanks again for helpin'. We're doin' fine. Nice weather. Andi's lookin' for a job."

Another message from Hollofield: "Charleston's good. Lots of people, tourists, so I can get outside. I'm like invisible. No one suspicious. No one watching me. This gay guy, Scott, leaves me alone. But I need to move out. Too much sex in the other bedroom. Uncomfortable. Not my style."

Morel joked: "Maybe he can convert you? Use a little wine on you? Get you good and fried?"

Hollofield: "UR kidding, right?"

Then, Morel watched as Andi drove right through the cemetery, parking close enough that Morel could see her car on the cinder road. *That's gutsy*, he thought. *But what if they're following her?*

She carried two packages across the graves, not even being courteous to the underneath dead. Morel held the wrought iron door open for her and she grunted as she set down the heavier grocery bag. "Got you some of your fav treats, Palm: Chips. Water. Some Little Debbies."

"Okay, but what are you eating?"

"I've got salads for both of us now. Later, I can pick up some burgers."

Morel frowned, but what could he do? Rehabbing now in a crypt, no running water, no electricity. "Andi, we gotta get outta here. This is no good."

Andi nodded, put her arms around his neck. "Listen big guy. This is fine for a day or two. I'm working on a job. I think I got it."

"What? Where?"

"I met some Italian guy, owns the flea market, the Pecan Pie, where I stopped for new clothes. Says he needs a waitress over at The Plum Puddin'."

"I bet he does. What's his name?"

"Goes by Domingo. Kind of a Italian stud."

***

It wasn't exactly a gauntlet, but Andi felt uncomfortable just the same. After her 4 pm hair appointment, she drove to The Plum Puddin'. The experience started absurdly. Walking up the stairs to the bar, she had to pass between five guys postioned on the stairs. Each one eyed her as she stepped up, one guy even touching her new hairdo, another guy looking up her short black skirt she got at the Pecan Pie.

Knowing these might be her co-workers, she forced a smile and reached the last step a bit worried. This was sexism and she didn't like it. Then, Domingo, the boss guy she met at the used clothes store, skipped over to meet her, putting his arm around her and moving her to a table by the bar.

"Hey, sexy thing. Happy you accepted my offer to interview. Great! Like your new hair. What's that called, streaking? Black with a little magenta. Good combo."

***

Domingo was a good-hearted guy with a preference for wild women. At first, he got the impression that Andi could be had. Thought for sure they'd be real close. But she reacted badly to being touched, didn't like flirty comments and backed off when he tried to chat her up. So, not wanting to lose a good thing immediately, he settled down, got to the business of hiring her. Maybe they'd hook up later.

"Andi, can you work today, right now? Want to start your training?"

"I need a job."

"Okay, okay, good. You like the set up here? Like the menu?"

Andi played it tight. "Maybe. Didn't like the welcome. Who are these guys? You like what they put me through?"

"No, no. You handled them right. Just right. Put them in their place. Listen. They're hard workers, macho, bus boys, cooks, you know, just guys who wanna be friendly. They'll be okay, they'll respect you now. I think you done good. Showed some professional attitude. That's why I like you. You got spunk."

"What job are you offering?"

"Well, be a waitress. Nights. Come in at about five, work until maybe two. How's that? Some overtime maybe. We split the tips, you know, but we get a rich crowd, you know, good tips, tourists and the regulars. Did you look us up on the internet? We get real good ratings, you know. The tops. Great food. Entertainment. You'll like it here."

"I need a place to stay. I live in a real dump now."

"Yeah, where? Downtown? Where ya at?"

"I need a better place. I got no money, well, just a little. I'd like a rental, but I can't pay yet. I'll have to wait for a few paychecks. You got any contacts, anybody who needs a house sitter, an empty rental apartment, some place I can stay for a while for free. I can't stay where I'm at. It's dangerous."

Domingo smiled, "Sure, sure. I got a place that's empty now. A nice place. Listen. This place is completely furnished. I can take you over there, show you around. Then, we'll work out some payments. I like you, like your style. Baby, I can tell you'll bring business in here once folks get to know you. You got high-class attitude with a made for lovin' body. Perfect combination."

Andi gave him that look again, that back off look, warning him. "Domingo, you listen. I'm not your baby. I'm not some piece of ass. I need a good job, good pay. I need a place to stay. You got it? I can look somewhere else."

Giving her that practiced shy smile, Domingo said, "No offense, really. I like you, that's all. Nothing more, okay? How 'bout I show you the basics here, get you a nice, plum colored uniform that fits, then I can show you my place over on Oglethorpe. You good with that?"

8
Boating

"I get the fuckin' picture. No problem."

The bare-bones home office in Chapel Hill on Franklin Street had no comfy couch for the lean, emaciated gunman, Crosby Haggart, out of Biloxi. He was ready to go.

"Take your time, my man. No final word given. Sit down. I'll get you a coffee," said Agent Edward Traynor, the gray-haired, aging local man, former Green Beret, Bay of Pigs operative, now seventy-three and a retired professor of history in this busy university town.

Haggart reluctantly slid down the wall near the kitchen, and sat on the floor, his long thin legs sticking out of his khaki shorts like toothpicks, a mean sneer on his green-tinted, unwashed face, his T-shirt proclaiming "Big Noise" on his chest. In the shadows he looked like Jim Carey after a botched liver transplant.

Part of the assassination team from Fort Bragg, he was used to taking down unnecessary problems with minimum expenditure. Haggart's one failure was Palmer Morel. Just a little off on his shot from the helicopter over the Haw River. Morel was hit but survived.

Traynor brought a mug of black coffee and a hard donut on a paper plate.

Haggart grabbed the coffee, rejected the donut. "So, if you have no plan, I do."

"Knew you would. Tell me just a little." Traynor pulled over an old, hump-backed kitchen chair, sat near Haggart, in front of the bright window, his face in shadows.

Haggart said, "Listen. No dead body. No noise. No news stories. Morel will just disappear."

"What…just kill him, put him on a boat, sink him in the ocean like Osama bin Laden?" Traynor smiled his sarcasm.

A sip of hot coffee and Haggart smiled too, an ugly smile, twisted but meaningful. "You got it. Morel's hiding out in Savannah. Got a contact in the cemetery. He found Morel. Watches him for me. He's in some crypt by the river. Easy access at night. Small boat. Make him dead. Take the body to the boat. Anchor Morel deep off the coast. No trace. A simple disappearance."

Traynor: "Where's the crypt?"

Haggart: "In that cemetery."

Traynor: "How many men?"

Haggart: "Some."

Traynor: "Weapon?"

Haggart: "You don't need to know."

***

A line of condos, old, red-brick, all connected by mortar and affluence. This was **Oglethorpe Ave.**, across the avenue from historic Colonial Cemetery, the neatly-kept, lovely, old resting place. Much different from Bonaventure, Colonial was a place to walk in the sunshine, not in the shadows of Spanish moss as at Bonaventure Cemetery.

The poet Conrad Aiken had lived on **Oglethorpe** until tragedy and needless death interrupted his young life. Murder-suicide. Both mom and dad gone in one night. The deaths gave Oglethorpe an eerie feel, especially at night.

Near this home was an almost identical townhouse, on the market now, but still completely furnished. Domingo was trying to sell it, had a few offers, but he only wanted to sell it at his price. Why lose money if he could make the payments on it for awhile?

He waited outside the home for Andrea York, his new, attractive waitress. Dealing with her had been difficult. Prickly and precise, she needed this job but kept pushing him away. Yes, he knew she had a boyfriend. Yes, she was insistent that he keep his hands off her. But he couldn't.

Helping her with her uniform had been too tempting. Yes, he had to touch her. Yes, she slapped him gently but forcefully when he touched her ass. But still he felt he had a chance with her. When did he ever fail?

He watched now as her little red car went by, then made a u-turn to park behind his car. He waited for her as she approached, the new short skirt revealing shapely, strong legs. He smiled at her, but she remained totally, totally serious.

"This it?" she asked, looking up at the three storey home.

"Yep."

"It's big."

"Yep. Enough space here for your big boy friend, ya think?"

"Yep, I think he'll like it. When can we move in?"

Domingo, thought a moment. "Any time. I'll rent it to you for free until your second check. Then, I'll expect $1400 a month. Can you afford that?"

"Two weeks free, huh? Well, if my boy friend can't get his money transferred from Chapel Hill, I guess we can move back out? No rent fee?"

"Sure, sure. I'll get you started here. Like I said, it's vacant. I'm trying to sell it. Two weeks. Shit, maybe you can find somewhere more affordable then, huh? Just glad to help you out."

"Okay, show me the inside."

***

The tan, older model, Grand Marquis, contained three, but thin, muscular men, all dressed alike: black shorts, black T-shirts, black Asics running shoes.

Inside the vast trunk were their weapons and a light-weight, inflatable boat, a Rover Rib, capable of holding three people if one of the people was lying on the floor of the boat, dead.

Timing was important. The Cuban contact in Savannah had been mowing the grass in the afternoon and assured them Morel would be asleep at midnight. The target had infrequent visitors: an Asian artist, a bulky athletic guy and a daily live-in companion, the Fort Bragg contact and lover, Andrea York.

Morel was prone to wander out of the crypt, both during the day and night, the contact reported, even though he probably knew it could be dangerous. But his bedtime was constant: eleven p.m. after some quality time with his lover. Today he had sat outside for about an hour after exercising on the paths, walking slowly, his injuries still holding his activity to a minimum.

Counting on a little deviation of Morel's schedule, the team would be able to carry out their mission sometime after midnight. The site for the boat launch had already been picked out, the path to Morel's crypt had been mapped, and a slick plastic sled to pull across the cemetery lawn to the inflated boat was assessed and approved. Fifteen minutes tops. Two men for the kill. One man at the boat dock rendezvous.

A short trip by inflatable boat. The body then attached to the heavy steel plate. The body overboard and disappeared. Half hour.

As the quiet group drove toward highway 95, Haggart checked his watch. Six p.m. An easy six hours to their destination.

***

The new place was good and Andi felt it was time to move into the red-brick apartment. Palmer seemed better, but restless, his legs a little weak, the bandages still on his wounds, but he needed to get away from the cemetery. Much too boring for him now. Kinda dangerous, him getting antsy, walking around outside, talking to the visitors, talking to the workers.

After her first bit at the Plum Puddin', she got Domingo to go with her at 11:30 p.m., down the long rustic road to Bonaventure, the moss hanging low in the evening fog. Domingo liked her. She knew his background, his reasoning. And she had him now, like a pet goat.

She texted Morel about her plan and told him to wait out near the cemetery gate, and he did, dragging his stuff in the backback across the lawn. Andi beeped the little horn on her red KIA and Palmer waved.

She stuffed Domingo in the small back seat for now, and let Palmer stretch his legs in front. "How ya doin' big boy?" she asked. "Ready for some after midnight city lights?"

Morel seemed confused, but optimistic. "I guess, but just when I was getting comfortable, you're taking me away?"

"Yeah, why not? Hey, in the backseat, meet my new boss. Johnny Domingo."

Morel half turned, stuck out his hand, "Thanks, man. We owe you one."

Domingo muttered, taking Morel's handshake, "No problem. Glad to help out." But under his breath he mumbled to himself. *I don't like this fuckin' blond dude.*

***

After parking the Grand Marquis near the pavilion at Honey Park, Haggart and his buddies took the boat to the dock, inflated it, and set it in the Wilmington River. Gently climbing on board, Haggart and Joe Bobri from Rocky Mount set off, using the paddles at first, leaving Mark Hanford, formerly of Baton Rouge, behind.

The fuckin' little boat bobbed irrationally on the surface of the river, its sluggishly-bouncy motion toward Bonaventure Cemetery affecting the morale of the two men. Impatient, Haggart started the motor and the boat bucked high and took off into the night.

Haggart yelled above the motor's roar, "It's okay. We're good."

Dobri wasn't so sure, "We're late. We need speed."

Without much trouble, the boat moved north against the water, gained speed and Haggart shifted to high speed, the boat now skimming fast, maintaining contact with the water intermittingly. Dobri held on tight.

"There it is," hollered Haggart, spotting the shoreline off Bonaventure Cemetery.

"Goddam, we getting'too close. Cut the motor. We'll paddle," yelled Dobri.

Haggart cut the juice, the boat slowed more, and the men dug into the water with the small paddles. There were no lights on shore, just a line of trees, one with a dangling piece of white cloth.

Dobri clicked his flashlight, scanned the shore and found the marked tree. Haggart turned the wheel, aiming straight for the target, then propelled the boat vigorously toward shore with his short paddle.

Securing the boat using the nylon rope and a single spike, the men grabbed their hand guns, struggled up the bluff and jogged toward the Mitchell crypt.

Arriving first, Dobri clicked on his flashlight and revealed the wrought iron doorway, wide-open to the night.

Catching up, Haggart looked inside and groaned, "The fuckin' son of a bitch is not here!"

9

The Camera Man

Of course, the beauty of Savannah takes away your fears, not that the warmth and gorgeous colors blind you entirely. Not that exactly. But this Georgia city seemed like a protective oasis, far from the busy, busy, busy-ness of the Raleigh Triangle, far from drive-by shootings in Durham and crowded highways and long drives to Chapel Hill for restaurants, then drives to Raleigh for dramatic theater, then back to Chapel Hill, then to Durham for Bulls' games. The constant need to go somewhere, looking for entertainment, for a new restaurant, a new thrill.

Here, Savannah offered history, a southern reverie, slow-moving tourists who had a lot of time.

Morel looked out the open window of his new townhome onto Oglethorpe. It was noon. Tourists were walking by, some guy had set up a large camera outside on the grass in middle of Oglethorpe Avenue, snap, snap, snapping photos of Corad Aiken's old house near Morel's rental home.

And the smell in the air was deep-south, deeper-south than Chapel Hill and Raleigh and deeper still than Carolina's Pinehurst and Fayetteville. And everything moved slowly in the heat.

Andi was sleeping late, a light cover over her curvy nude body. Morel felt confident in their love now, and wished the nightmare of Feds trying to find him didn't exist. Morel loved Savannah and knew he could stay here forever if he could just survive.

He took another step toward the window. The huge oaks, the light breeze, the intoxicating aroma of this oasis. If that guy with the camera would stop looking at him through the window. If that guy stopped staring at him.

***

With little money coming in and her lover Palmer Morel off with some seductive therapist, former stripper Cat Gallaher was pissed, her red-hair blazing in the autumn light from the kitchen window.

Sure, she kept Morel's three-year-old son TJ for leverage. Sure she had no right to the kid, but she and Morel had been taking care of him together for two years and that freakin' Morel better know she'd never part with him without some big bucks. Their lovely town home in

Deerington Village was shouting with emptiness: no Morel to tease her, no Morel to play toy trains with TJ, no Morel in her arms.

How could he fall for that physical therapist? Cute and smart he had told her. Cute and smart? Shit, she was twelve years younger than Morel. What did she know about real love, sacrifice? Cat took out her cell and dialed Morel's number down in Savannah. She didn't care if the freakin' FBI was bugging their phones.

***

Something was bugging her husband, and Mrs. Joanna Morel didn't like it. He was just getting over a slight stroke that left him dizzy some times, and now his only son, Palmer, was knee deep in trouble down in the Carolinas.

Then her husband James got some crazy phone call a couple days ago. Very short. And he wouldn't talk about it. It reminded her of the past when he'd get a call and went to go off to some gun show over in St. Louis or Kansas City or Detroit. Always said it was his buddy Eugene Folger from back in his Viet Nam days, wanting to reconnect, tell war stories. But now it happened again. She had thought Eugene had died.

So, after the call, her 78-year-old spouse immediately started sending his son photocopies of all that JFK assassination stuff from the

1970s, all those letters from congressmen on the Select Committee. Mrs. Morel thought her husband was over that foolishness, but now Palmer had been shot, and he was in hiding. Why did he need JFK information?

The FBI was looking for him and her own home in Sedalia was being watched, her phone probably tapped. She decided to text a message to her son:

Palmer, your dad is very upset about you. He got some phone call from Eugene again, I think. Set him off. I'm trying to stop him but he's determined to fly down to see you. He's still not right from his stroke. He wants to help but he's taking his guns. Look out for him when he flies down, okay? Don't let him do nothin' stupid.

***

Cameras were Joey Lingua's cup of tea. He was good with guns, with union-busting, with the women at the strip club, and standing out here by some dead poet's house doing spy duty was fun.

But he was bored. *Can't I even take a photo oft him in the window?* he texted his boss. *No*, was the answer. *We must wait. Just watch.*

So he pretended some more, moved the camera, flirted with some young women walking by and tried to keep his spirits up. He wondered if Morel was getting suspicious.

The guy kept looking out the window at him, nervous as hell. Then, some girl appeared in the window next to Morel. Looked like she had just draped a sheet over her body or something.

Then the freakin' sheet fell off her breasts and Joey got an eyeful. *Dammit, that woman is hot!* Against the rules, he quickly moved his camera toward the window, he clicked off two—three--four photos before the couple moved away. *Dynamite!*

***

Andi was just being playful, not serious about sex now. Besides, Morel had enough of her last night. Tired her out. She had to get ready for work, get on that plum uniform they required, do something better with her hair. She hated the new hairdo, too short and those magenta streaks were just simply obnoxious.

Morel still tried to capture her for more sex, but she escaped the big lug and ran into the shower, locking the door. She had only 45 minutes to get ready and go. Then, Morel's cell phone started ringing on top of the sink where he musta left it. Shit! Sloppy wet with soap, she slipped out of the shower and grabbed the phone.

And she quickly got an earful. Morel's last lover, the ex-stripper Cat Gallaher, was yelling at her, telling her where to go, telling her to back off, Morel was her girl. And, what's more, if Morel wanted to see his kid any time soon, Andi should get the hell outta Savannah and back to Chapel Hill unless she wanted to get hurt.

Cat said she didn't care if Andi were some kinda athletic superwoman, Cat would break her face so she wouldn't be so cute any more. After the Cat demon hung up, Andi stood there in the middle of the bathroom floor, soapy suds dripping down her body to the floor. Then. Morel opened the bathroom door, his blue eyes real bright, his hands all over her soapy body. God dammit, she was gonna be late for work!

***

The plane in Kansas City was late. James Morel hated to fly, he was too old for this shit, but his son was mixed up with something bad out in North Carolina and he had to get there to take care of it. His buddy Eugene had given him another extreme job.

In an hour he was looking out the airplane's window over St. Louis, pondering his plans. After sending his son all the JFK assassination stuff a few weeks ago, as a warning, Palmer had left the hospital and gone into hiding. No problem there. He was in danger. Maybe he learned something from that JFK history. For one, don't be over-confident. For another, trust no one, especially any females placed close to you to watch you. His grandson TJ was also at risk and Mr. Morel could not allow that.

Touching down at RDU after a bumpy flight, the elder Morel got a cab and took off for Deerington Village. He'd talk to that slut, Cat Gallaher, and take possession of TJ. She could go back to the Italian mob and do some more lap dancing. He could not care less.

Then he had to find Palmer and take him back to Sedalia. The FBI had no true need to kill Palmer. They just thought they did. Mr. Morel would set them straight.

10

Punked Out

The Plum Puddin' off Reynolds Square was running a smooth lunch hour, the process working well except at Andi's station. Where was she?

Domingo had to do all the back bar stuff himself, and Andi's station had to be worked by Brianna Taylor, the 22-year-old waitress with short, bleached-blonde hair and a punker attitude. She didn't mind at first, could use the extra tips, but she began to resent it.

She knew Andi had that live-in boy friend who musta been high-maintenance. She always came to work out of breath and with that freakin' afterglow of sex on her cheeks. And she knew Domingo had the hots for her too.

Brianna had dated Domingo for awhile last year, but he was always looking for someone new. Shit! And on the trip back to the bar to get the drinks for table 5, there was Domingo chatting up Andi who had just arrived, out of breath, of course. She did look hot. She couldn't really blame Domingo, but, shit, this was the workplace, dammit! Didn't he know not to mix work with pleasure? Who cares if most dating studies showed that tons of people meet their spouses at work. Domingo should rise above all that stuff.

Then, glancing down at the bar to get her drinks Domingo had placed there, she saw a hand-written note. She picked it up. Domingo's note had Andi's name and a phone number. Hmm. She'd take that number and maybe do some prank calls to Andi tonight. That'd shake the bitch up.

***

At first, Morel didn't want to answer his phone. It might be the FBI, Army intelligence, somebody checking to see if he were home. The photographer had made him way too nervous, and with Andi at work he had no back-up plan. No way to get away from the townhome.

But he picked up anyway. Luckily, it was just his dad having a fit up in Raleigh. *Where is that Gallaher slut?* he wanted to know. *I'm down here to get TJ and take him back to Sedalia. Where in hell are you, Palmer?*

Palmer relaxed a little, talking softly. *Dad, I'm okay. TJ's okay. Really. Cat makes a good mom. I know she got stuck with him, but we're* under too much pressure here to have TJ with us here in Savannah. And you shouldn't take him to Sedalia either. He likes Cat. He'll be very upset.

Mr. Morel let out a big *humph*! on that one. *So, you and this new woman are shacked up down there in Savannah and have no time for TJ. That it? No time for your own kid?*

Palmer tried explaining. *Dad, dad. Andi's my therapist. She's taking care of me. She works hard and pays the bills. She's taking a big chance hanging out with me. She's absolutely great. My body is getting much better. I'm walking, and eating well. But, dad. You're taking a bigger chance calling me. Your phone might be bugged, you know.*

But Mr. James Morel was not to be deterred. *I'm driving down there today. You meet me somewhere. Maybe back at that cemetery. We can talk there and I can meet that Andi person. And just shut up. I'm coming today. I'll be at that Bonaventure gate at 8 pm.*

***

Getting in touch with Joey Lingua was easy, but Domingo had always tried to avoid dealing with the mob. Getting a text message from Joey shook him up. What the fuck did he want? They were grade school buddies, sure, but in high school Joey got mobbed-up fast, his whole family was involved: strip clubs in the burbs, the veggie market downtown, interstate gambling, prostitution out on Tybee Island, the trollies, and all those vending machines. They had contacts everywhere, but what did they have with Domingo? Nothing.

God, his text scared him. *Meet me at the Lucas Theater.* Just that simple. *Meet me there at 10 pm.* How could he? Nights were busy. A great jazz group would be playing in the basement. He had fucking work to do.

Yet, that was just like Joey. Domingo could see him, the dark hair receding, strong shoulders, a camera always nearby. A hobby he always said. A hobby for what? Taking nude photos? Jesus, he had to wait till 10 pm. He had time to think about the meeting. Should he pack a gun?

He fingered his phone, then typed a brief message to Joey, *Okay.* He wondered who was performing at the Lucas Theater. Was it the 50s musical review again? And what the fuck did Joey have to do with the theater?

***

Back in Deerington Village, drama queen Cat Gallaher's anger increased. But Morel's phone was busy. She tried again. Busy. Fuck!

She picked up TJ and made a decision. She'd go to Savannah. Going to her computer, she set TJ down on the couch.

Why? What doing? he complained.

On-line, she found a Savannah motel easily on the southside just past the airport. A couple of clicks and she had rented a two bedroom on the first floor. She could be down there in six hours.

She grabbed TJ, picked up his box of toys, and marched out to her car. She got TJ in his seatbelt in the back seat of the Shelby, took out his old Gameboy and gave him a small box of Cheetos. He smiled and said *Gud.*

Pulling out onto the street, she spotted a big black Lexus as it moved away from the curb and started to follow her.

Jesus Christ! Couldn't they give her a break? Well, she knew the backroads to the mall, she knew some interesting twists in the road, and she'd lose those fuckers.

Heading south on 15/501, she turned east and took the shortcut south to highway 64. The Lexus had to wait for some traffic and then took off after her, but she was pushing 70 mph on the 55 mph back road, then hit the brakes, quickly swerving off at Big Hole Road. She waited, and then turned back east to 15/501 after the black Lexus passed her by.

But her Mustang shimmied wildly in the turn, catching some gravel, then straightened out and plowed on, leaving a huge dust trail behind her. Unfortunately, her hurried exit could be easy to follow, if they found out she ditched them.

11

Nature Boy

Morel made a decision. He had to get out of his townhome. He was really, really bored. Andi was gone a long time each day, and he felt strong enough to get a job, too.

His tennis was rusty, he couldn't use his real name, but there must be a tennis club in Savannah that would hire him as an attendant or desk clerk or something.

He took a quick shower, put on his black shorts and a T-shirt that said *Nature Boy*.

He turned on the computer. "Savannah Tennis Clubs" he Googled. Up popped five nearby and a few scattered out in the burbs. He ran off a copy, grabbed his phone and limped down the steps into the sunshine. *God, this feels great!* he thought.

A block away to the north was Oglethorpe Square on Abercorn, some tourists resting on the benches, birds chirping in the trees. He found a vacant bench and punched in a number for the Old Elm Racquet Club. No answer. He hit repeat. No answer. *Three times the charm,* he thought. Still no answer.

He went down the list and found another club, The Rickety Post, off Skidaway Road near Bacon Park. *Hmm. Sounds cool. Lots of moss covered trees, a little creek, and sure enough a rickety gate.*

He punched in the number and a gal with a southern-fried voice purred, "The Rickety. How can I help you?"

Morel paused. What kinda job did he want? He couldn't apply for the pro job. His credentials would give him away. So, he stated a lesser goal.

"Hi, I'm Rick Samson. I'm looking for one of those jobs you advertised at the Tennis Club."

There was no answer immediately, then… "We have a few openings in our kitchen and wait staff. Did you see our ad in the newspaper?"

Morel grunted, "Yeah, ah, who do I talk to about signing up for one of those?"

The young lady paused again and then said, "Well, if you get here by five, I could interview you."

Morel checked out the time… 3:30. "Okay, I'll be there right away. Who should I ask for?"

"I'm Violet. I'll be at the main desk when you come in. And, oh, bring some references."

"References?" Morel sighed. "Uh, I'm from Chapel Hill and left my stuff back there. Can I send them to you after the interview?"

Violet was reassuring, "Sure, sure. You sound nice enough and we're kinda desperate for help this fall. Lots of our seasonal workers just went back to college. But bring me some names from previous jobs, okay?"

***

Taking a little break in the back room of The Plum Puddin', Andi chewed on a salad and checked her cel phone. Nothing from Palmer.

One message from her buddy, Lori, back in Chapel Hill. She was gonna run the Charlotte Half Marathon in October. She wanted Andi to come over, spend the weekend. There'd be a big party, lots of guys.

Andi had to think about that one. She had work to do and leaving Palmer alone was not an option. The big guy was doing fine now, but he got lonely. She was his only contact.

Plus, how could he shop or go outside for anything? They were under siege. She suspected everyone, and Palmer would be so vulnerable. No one as back-up.

She punched in his number and waited. Morel quickly picked up and gave his usual greeting as her name spelled out on his cel, "Hello, plum lady, what's up?"

Andi smiled. "I'm worried about you. Miss you. Were you taking a nap?

Morel chuckled, "Not exactly. I'm out looking for a job."

The line got quiet and Andi could hear the noise of traffic. "What job? You need to be back home. What the hell are you doing?"

Shifting in his seat, Morel spoke crisply, "I got a chance for a job at a tennis club is all. Don't worry. I'm in a cab. No one's following. Hey,
I just had to do something. You're gone all day. I'm really bored. I gotta get back my life."

Perplexed, she began pacing around the back room, nervously making circles in her hair. "Palmer, don't do it. You're not ready. You'll get tired. And you're not safe."

"Listen, I'll be fine. I'll apply for the job, go home and take a nap. And, anyway, my dad called. He's driving down from Chapel Hill today. He's worried about me and TJ. I gotta meet him at 8 pm this evening over at Bonaventure. I'm taking care of business."

Then, the line went dead. Andi redialed but Morel either couldn't or wouldn't pick-up. "Son of a bitch," she whispered to herself.

***

Out at his strip club across the bridge to Hardeeville, Joey got on his computer, transferred the photos, and saw they turned out bitchin'. There was Morel looking out his window on the second floor. Next to him was Morel's woman barely covered by the sheet.

Then the sheet fell off and Morel reached over to touch her breast. They moved away from the window and the last photo showed her bare back with Morel's arm around her. Great moment.

In a few minutes Joey had sent the photos off to his FBI contact. He had done his part, but the job was screwy. If the FBI wanted Morel dead, why couldn't Joey just pop him through the open window?

The noise of traffic would stifle the small zip of the gun's silencer, he could quickly breakdown the tripod and camera, walk across the Oglethorpe Avenue divider to his car and leave the scene. Easy. But the FBI didn't operate like the mob. Too convuluted, no trust, no practicality. Shit! Said they still wanted to use Morel somehow. More games.

He was tired of these games, and they wanted him back at Morel's place tonight, using some fancy, night-vision camera, looking for visitors, taking photos. Well, he'd add something new to the mix. A sex plan of his own.

He hoped Domingo would be on time at The Lucas Theater. Taking Domingo with him would give him some protection, a back-up guy to take the photos of any visitors at the outside entrance on Oglethorpe.

Then he'd work his devious plan as well. He'd get Domingo to make a loud disturbance, then have him run into Colonial Cemetery across from Oglethorpe. Wouldn't have to tell Domingo what he'd be doing inside. Morel would go outside to investigate. and Joey would get inside the apartment somehow through the alley with enough time to get real close to Morel's gorgeous girl friend.

He loved the sight of her firm body, her decadent hairstyle, her pouty mouth. Just five minutes with her was all he'd need. Domingo could keep Morel occupied for at least that long. He looked at his nude photo of her again. Jesus, she was perfect.

***

The candy-apple-red Buick Lucerne rental was perfect in most ways, but its silent ride was too quiet, too smooth, and James Morel was getting too groggy, tired, sleepy on his long journey.

He opened the windows. Maybe a little breeze would help him wake up. He was still on time to Savannah to meet Palmer at 8 pm, but at his age he required frequent restroom stops and needed a short walk each time to get the kinks out of his legs and brain.

Traveling on I-95 could be treacherous for an old guy, too, big trucks, speeding cars, too many lanes. He tried to play it safe, staying in the far right lane, but the merging traffic often forced him to slow down, be very alert, and when those big rigs pushed him from behind he got frightened and often felt the risk of an accident. He tried not to admit it it, but he did get a bit confused at times since his stroke.

Maybe he was getting too old for these tasks. Used to be, one call from his buddy from his Nam days and he'd be ready to roll. Go take out any guy needed to be eliminated. Even his kids and wife knew nothing of these episodes. He'd just say he was goin' to a gun convention in St. Louis and his wife would accept it with only a groan. She thought he was a only gun nut, but he wasn't. He was an enforcer for military ops.

About one hour from Savannah, nearing Charleston, he pulled onto the off-ramp to get some gas and a Coke. He needed some caffeine and maybe a cheap slice of pizza. At least the cheese would be hot and fresh he hoped.

After filling the tank and using his debit card for the gas and the pizza stuff, James set the food packet on the passenger seat, went to the back of the Buick and opened the trunk.

He had a license to conceal-carry, but he preferred to keep his pistols in a gym bag in the trunk. Sure, he thought about not having them handy in the front seat, but he wasn't just some gun nut.

He'd always carry one of them in a shoulder holster during those trips through the bad side of towns. Didn't need 'em at all in Sedalia except for Friday nights when the honky tonks like "Rumours" were open a couple blocks away on Main Street. Then he'd carry the 4 inch baby in his jacket pocket if he needed to go out for milk and bread. Course his wife worried, but he explained he was keepin' her safe.

Now, he picked out the .25 baby, checked if it was locked and loaded, stuck it in his pants pocket. These guns were purchased back in 1968 as a set, a Browning factory-cased set. Got 'em all for $750. Now they'd be worth near $3000. Carrying it, he felt more confident. Some

FBI agent try to stop him and Palmer, well the FBI guy'd be lookin' into the barrel of a .25 baby Browning.

And, at close range, the gun was powerful enough to take out any female operative whose usefulness was over.

12

Rickety Post

Palmer's little boy, TJ, was not responding well to the detour back to Chapel Hill. After the fiasco of turning off onto Big Hole Road, Cat Gallaher had been unable to keep her Shelby Mustang out of the ditch and the Feds were on her like a warm bucket of molasses.

TJ lost his Cheetos and his toy trains in the water after the muddy ditch seeped into the backseat. A little shook up, he was okay, held tightly in his little seat-belted chair. So was Cat.

But the whole idea of getting down to Savannah and confronting Morel was quashed. Now TJ sat on a hard-backed oak chair outside the office in some Federal building in downtown Chapel Hill, the sun was shining too brightly into his eyes from the big window, and Cat herself was fuming mad at the whole deal. TJ had been given an old, rusty pair of handcuffs to play with, but his young mind couldn't get over the shock of not seeing his dad again. Cat had promised him.

Cat had said that his daddy was not in the sky in heaven, but had come down to earth again. And at McIntyre's, TJ had seen his dad resurrected for a brief moment.

But now, no dad, no toys, no Cheetos. For her part, Cat refused to talk to authorities; she had called a lawyer recommended by the Deerington Village consortium, yet she was still stuck with the Feds until her lawyer could propel himself to Chapel Hill from Durham.

She wasn't under arrest. She was just being detained, whatever that meant. And her refusing to answer anything about Palmer Morel was not sitting too well with the big boys.

At least they had her beautiful Ford Shelby towed over to Cole Park Plaza. Besides one busted tire and a front fender too crumpled against the tire to allow it to be driven, her car was fine, fine, just fine! It would be fixed by tomorrow. But shit! She had thought she was making progress seeing Morel but now she didn't have many options at all.

Morel was still hiding out with that DPT sex toy, Andrea York, TJ was still crying outside the door, and her hope for some sort of normality was an ever distant impossibility.

***

The Georgia afternoon was perfectly normal, humid, but very hot, and business at the Tennis Club on Skidaway Road was extremely slow. Even the old geezers had canceled their doubles.

Thirty-five-year-old Violet Broughton, brown hair under a blue tennis cap, looked out the Tennis Club's front window, her little butt peeking out of her short white skirt, as she watched the "Mom's Taxi Service" dark-silver vehicle pull around the circle driveway of The Rickety Post and stop just outside her window. The afternoon was winding down and she would get off work in half an hour.

Her last task was to interview Rick Samson, some guy who called wanting a job. Said he was middle-aged, and out of work. He seemed complicated on the phone, something about his answers hesitant and contrived, and Violet was curious about him: was he some doper looking for a temp job, was he a tourist out of money needed for a flight back home, was he some wandering klutz searching Savannah because he had read "Midnight in the Garden of Good and Evil"?

As she watched, the guy paid the cabby, and she observed the rather tall, muscular man, with blond hair, wearing white tennis clothes with a shirt that read "Nature Boy."That seemed odd apparal for an interview. It also seemed strange he had no tan at all. Long legs as white as a baby's butt. He slammed the cab door shut and turned abruptly toward the club entrance.

She ducked away from the window to avoid his gaze, and then proceeded to the front desk of the tennis club to meet the mystery man. He was reading the court schedule at the main desk, his elbows supporting him, as she walked over to meet him.

"Hello, Mr. Samson. I'm Violet Broughton," she called out, right hand raised to shake his hand.

Samson slowly raised his head and stood straight, his light blue eyes meeting hers, his big paw enveloping her hand. "Ma'am, pleased to meet you."

His politeness seemed sincere, his wide smile bright, revealing openness and good humor. He handed her a small white notecard. "Here's the names and phone numbers of some folks back in Chapel Hill. If you call, they'll give me a good report, I hope." He smiled again, and as she took the card she noticed he did not wear a wedding ring.

"Well, thank ya so much. Did you want some lemonade? We can chat over by the bar if ya'd like?" Violet led him over to a table near the bar. Morel sized her up quickly: about 5' 8", strong tennis legs under that short white tennis dress, graceful walk, blue tennis cap, dark brown hair, and very erect posture, almost like a model. *Must be about middle thirties*, he surmised.

He took a seat as she went to the bar and brought back two big glasses of lemonade. "These are sweetened, hope ya don't mind," she said.

"Not at all. I need a cool drink right now. It's in the nineties out there." He smiled again and his blue eyes had their usual effect.

Violet coughed, almost choking as she tried to reply. Putting down her drink, she swallowed hard. "Can you excuse me for a second," she said as she rushed back to the bar for some napkins. Still coughing, she said, "Oh, dear me." Tears came to her eyes and she tried to compose herself. "You know, honey, I think I've met you before, haven't I? Have you played professional tennis on the tour?"

Samson shook his head. "Well, not on tour, but I've played some."

Violet nodded. "Yes, you have. Cuz I know. I saw you play in Columbus, Ohio, about five years ago. You only used them ol' wooden Jack Kramer racquets, didn't you? A novelty. Watched you lose in the finals. I had a front seat. You threw me your sweaty wrist bands. You're not really Mr. Samson, are ya, hon? Cuz I'd never forget those eyes of yours. You're Palmer Morel, aren't ya?"

***

"I need you to work later tonight," Domingo said. "I gotta an errand to do at 9:30. Should be done by 11:00. Okay?"

Andi frowned, looked at her watch, but what could she do? "Okay, 11:00. I can do that. But I thought you'd be here for the jazz bash. The Ben Tucker Trio. You love those old Johnny Mercer tunes, don't you?"

"Hate to miss it, hate miss it, I really do, but this can't wait. Maybe I'll still get a chance to hear part of it."

Andi finished moving the chairs and tables away from the piano and finally ended up with enough space for three more musicians. The space was tiny, but the customers wouldn't mind. Good jazz, good food and drink. What could be better?

She dialed Morel again and waited, but he didn't answer. He was ignoring her. She began to get edgy. She had trusted their relationship, but this secrecy bothered her. Why didn't he talk with her about getting a job? He was way too impulsive. Sure, he was bored, but why jeopardize everything?

Of course, even their romance had been rushed. Instant attraction. Impulsive. That was just like Morel. Escaping from Chapel

Hill. Living in a cemetery. And now him busting out of their new home on some whim. She knew all about his past, but this relationship still surprised her. On one level, she wished she wasn't so involved. She shoulda kept
her distance. Now, there'd be no way she could ever kill him. She wondered if she should call her contact and get outta this contract.

She had never left a job for some man before. No man was ever gonna own her. She loved her work, liked the secrecy and temptation of the special ops secrecy at night, enjoyed doing rehab on legs, hips, shoulders during the day.

Her pay at the Center had been excellent. Sure, the hours were long and she had to cajole and push her patients to do their therapy. But she loved the interaction, the real empathy she felt with her patients. Some of them still kept in touch on "Facebook," even though she could not reply.

This Morel affair kinda wrecked all that. Really, she couldn't blame just him. Both of them had been obsessed with each other, couldn't keep their hands off each other. So, now they were stuck. And she could never reveal her real first reason for creating the intimacy. Never.

But days like today made her wish she could dump special ops, leave Morel, get back to Deerington Village, doing the job she was trained for, having a professional career with no man to look after, no man to worry about. She had her patients and that had seemed enough responsibility. She had her friends, she had her running regimen, and she enjoyed all the evenings partying with some regular male friends, without the intrigue, no terrorists, violence and death.

Morel didn't want more kids. Said one was enough. And she didn't get a chance to bond with his son Tony Jack. Morel's ex-girl, the stripper, kept TJ all to herself.

She wondered *where's the future in all this? Is there any way out?*

***

Violet was saying, "I don't think we can use ya at the Club. We got hundreds of members. They'd all notice ya. It's not like you're a small guy I can hide and disguise. They'd spot ya easily; ask around. Your secret would be out. I mean, gracious, our patrons are really involved in Savannah, they go everywhere, know lots of important people. We've got members here from the Hunter Army Airfield base. Goodness. We've got police detectives. Government men. We have ladies on the make and ya'd be a target for some of their desires. Hell, I'd be interested in ya if I knew ya were available. All the women would. So, if you're in trouble, ya can't hope to hide here, honey."

Morel sipped his lemonade, nodded, tried to think of a good argument. Couldn't. "Well, I wanted to be straight with you. I have been hiding out. I don't really know why they're after me, I really don't. They think I know some secret stuff, but I don't. And I gotta do something. But, you know, I can't just sit all day. I'm getting healthy now. I'm feeling good. I could work in the back, do dishes, anything. I'd be sorta hidden, right?"

Violet shook her head. "Nope. I'd like ya here but the distraction? Think of it. I'd be worried every day. Tell ya what, sweetie. I got an idea. My friend Molly Lingua owns the Drayton Trolley Company. They do day and night tours. Might take ya on as tour guide.

Morel objected, "Wait. Wait. That'd be even more out in the open, don't ya think? Why don't I just be a tour driver?"

Violet said, "No, y'all wait. Before ya argue, listen to me. Ya know there's only tourists on board. Right? No locals or Feds. You'd tell stories about the historic places and all. You've got a good voice. Might be better if ya were a guide, wear some kinda funky clothes. Listen. Being a tour guide is better. If ya drove the trolley, you'd need picture ID, insurance, truck license all that stuff. Ya can't reveal all that, can ya, and stay hidden?"

"Maybe. Maybe, but I can't be a guide. I don't know Savannah. Shit, I'm used to coaching tennis. I'm not a circus barker."

"Well, ya have a good voice, ya have poise and y'all be given a script to memorize. Ya don't do the research yourself, silly. It's all very programmed. Just add your delightful personality. No problem."

Morel wondered, "Personality, huh. Shit, it would be all new. Standing up there with a microphone, dealing with history buffs, tourists. It's not me."

" But lots of advantages, too. You'd be out and about, not trapped, cooped up. I think I can get Molly to pay you in cash. She does that sometimes. No paperwork unless she gets picky. Then the deal would be off, of course. Wadda ya think, sweetie? Should I call her?"

Morel smiled, "Okay, it's all I got. Let's give it a shot."

Not able to resist, Molly stood up and smiled. "Great. I'll call her. Come over here. Give me a hug."

Returning her smile, Morel got up, and Violet jumped into his arms. "I've been wanting to hug y'all for about five years," she said.

13

Moon River

Deerington Village was a carnival of activity as the dispirited Cat Gallaher rode in the backseat of the yellow courtesy van from the body shop at Cole Park Plaza. The older driver was chatting away about beautiful sunsets he had seen, the variety to be had in Hawaii, the ominous setting sun before the hurricane hit New Orleans. The guy had been all over the world looking at freakin' sunsets and Cat was getting impatient. All she wanted was to get her car back.

Outside the window, the yellow bumblebee whirlygigs were pulsating in a circle, the blue tennis courts were full of youthful players, and walkers were working their bodies as a freshening in the air signalled the black clouds of an approaching storm. Little TJ was asleep in his car chair, his head resting on Cat's arm. Poor little kid. He missed his freakin' dad, and so did Cat.

Her over-heated brain couldn't accept that Morel was in Savannah without her, throwing her over for some therapist. Her heart ached to reunite with Morel. She really didn't want revenge. She understood it wasn't the therapist's fault. She must have got infatuated with Morel, looked into those blue eyes. He could have resisted, but he didn't. That was Palmer. Shit, he was totally unable to resist women.

The courtesy car pulled up to the front door of her garish townhome, the neon lights pulsating, the 1950s décor blatantly creating a party atmosphere. *Some party*, she thought. *Without Palmer the party is over.*

She thanked the driver, picked up TJ, slung him across her hip like a real mom, and tried to get the key into the front door. She missed a few times and nearly lost her temper. Then the key popped the door open, the cooling AC hit her face and she was home.

TJ was still sleeping so she put him down carefully on the living room couch. She walked down the hall and opened the fridge. There was still some cold beer, her favorite "Weeping Willow Wits" from Kinston, North Carolina, inside, and a half a salad from the local Harris Teeter. Lettuce, tomato, cucumbers, ham and thousand island.

She walked back to the living room and sat near the front window, chawing on her salad. She watched the neighbors play badminton in their side yard. Looked like fun. And, again, a shiver of loss moved through her body. When-oh-when would she get her Palmer back? When would they have this type of sporty fun?

She heard a distant thunder and she watched the walkers outside speed back home a little faster. The badminton game stopped and the men pointed toward the approaching storm. They quickly picked up the lawn chairs, the net and racquets and moved across the lawn toward the back deck. The families would be snug inside with their kids. Cat sipped at her beer, picked at her salad, trying hard to keep her own "wits" snug together.

***

The streets of Savannah were easy to follow once you learned it was all a big grid. James Morel came into the historic district with a few misconceptions. He thought the city might be run down a bit, as it was in the 1970s the last time he visited.

He noted the restoration of the big ante-bellum and Victorian homes, the fresh appearance of the restaurants, and he felt something else. Was it just the ambiance of the old South? Was it the exuberance caused by the many tourists strolling through the squares? Was it the lushness of the warm air, the slight breeze, the swaying trees?

He had enough time left to easily meet his son Palmer at Bonaventure Cemetery at 8 pm, so he parked the Buick on the street. It was just after five so he needn't fill the parking meter. According to the map he picked up at the tourist center, he was located on East Bay Street just beside a beautiful park near the river. Emmet Park invited him for a stroll, and he needed a good stretch of his legs.

The symmetry of the huge trees in the park provided a unique backdrop to the downtown area. Bars and restaurants across the street, large old buildings near Emmet Park. Walking toward the river, he came to a tall bluff with a narrow and dangerous staircase leading down to a cobbled roadway.

He wanted to go down to the riverfront, but the precipitous drop and narrow stairs stumped him. Instead, he turned away from the river and found a park bench, then sitting down and watching as trollies and horse-drawn carriages worked their way slowly on East Bay.

There were a few nice hotels across the street, too. He'd need a place to stay. Palmer had a townhome, but he didn't want to complicate an already messy situation. Best to stay down here later, near the river.

He studied the map, found Bonaventure Cemetery just off Skidaway Road. If he followed Bonaventure Road, it would lead right to the cemetery's front gate.

He'd like to get a beer. Maybe that would relax him. He got up, walked slowly to the crossing marker on the street, pushed the walk/wait button and stopped. He really liked this city. He wouldn't mind living here. Get away from the midwest. Soak up some southern culture.

The light changed and he walked past Tony Roma's Restaurant toward the Moon River Brewing Company. *God*, he thought. *"Moon River." What a great song.*

***

Andi was humming a Mercer tune, "Too Marvelous for Words," when a couple of big guys in suits walked over to the bar at the Plum Puddin'. Andi looked up from the table she was serving. Dark suitcoats now draped over the back of their chairs. Unusual suits for a hot summer day. And she immediately thought, *Feds, from up north.* Who wouldn't?

She finished placing the food at her table, told the two customers to "enjoy" and walked away from the bar toward the piano in the next area where she could still see the men.

Of course, they ordered soft drinks. One was talking to Domingo behind the bar. Domingo looked over her way and pointed at her. Oh damn. *Why'd he do that?* She ducked around the corner and waited, pretending to be busy cleaning tables.

But Domingo approached. He stopped behind her. "They wanna see you."

"Feds?"

"Yep."

"Think I can get outta here?"

"Nope."

"Goddam it. Wadda they want?"

"I think you know."

"Shit! I don't know anything!"

"Listen. Sit at that table over by the piano. I'm sending them to see you. Don't say nothin' if you don't want to. You have rights."

Andi put down the towel and sat at the table, her head down, her brain short-circuiting. Just a jumble of thoughts and images in her brain. Palmer nude in her bed. Her boss up in Chapel Hill asking her *why?* The hiding place at Bonaventure. The dark night as they had tried to sleep the first time in the cemetery, some owl asking *who?* The sharp, pointed hat pin she used to kill in Pittsboro.

The Feds knew how to saunter slow and easy, no hurry, their soft drinks in big glasses, lots of ice tinkling as they walked.

"Are you An—dray--ah?" the chunky, balding guy asked her, drawing out her name like some stupid ass.

***

It was a strange phone call Joey Lingua got earlier, at about 5 pm. His wife Molly called asking if he needed any more Trolley guides for the autumn. Sure he needed guides. All the freakin' college students were gone, it was nearing September and the tourists would still be coming hard until December.

What was wrong with her? Then, she wanted to know if he could pay this new guy in cash, as a favor to Violet. Jesus, Joey paid everybody in cash. That was the deal. No paper trail, no checks, no bank deposits except in small sums, and using cash from the strip joint to mingle it all together. Just like a laundramat. Confuse the IRS a little bit.

But then he asked who is this guy wants special treatment and Molly says he's in some kinda trouble. And Joey asks, you got his name, what's his name? And Molly says it's some tennis pro named Palmer Morel. *What the hell?*

So, after taking all those photos of Morel's townhome, getting some nude photos of his girl and trying to find out all about him, now Joey had the guy dropped right onto his lap.   He says quietly to Molly, sure. I'll hire him. Have him stop over to the trolley barn first thing
tomorrow morning. He can get one of the history scripts and start practicing. If he's got a good memory, good voice, he can work the "Ghastly Ghosts" Trolley at nights, 6 pm until 2 am. Be good for a mystery man at night. Who the fuck would recognize him?

Later, the next shift of girls comes into the joint to change for their topless duty at night and Joey feels great watching them take off their clothes. Big smile on his face and a few nude hugs. What a job! Plus, the freakin' FBI only needs some photos of Morel, but now he's gonna have Morel giving informational tours about Savannah ghosts!

Joey had to laugh. Some times his luck was just too damn good. He gets to supervise gorgeous young topless babes, gets to eat great food and he gets extra money for helping the FBI which gives him immunity for the prostitution that happens after hours. Plus, he'll get a fuckin' bonus for turning this Palmer Morel asshole over to the Feds. Jesus, it was almost enough to make him say a prayer of gratitude to the Lord. Almost.

***

"Please, God, please. Have Palmer pick up. Please, God!" And Andi's prayer was answered. Taking a cab back to their townhome, Palmer picked up.

"Andi, hey, I got a job."

But Andi frowned, didn't reply, waited.

"You there? I got a job. Did you hear me?

Once she started, it was hard for her to stop. "You got a job, a job, and I'm sitting down today with the FBI at work and they're quizzing me about you and all your illegal activities and how did you escape from the river, they thought you drowned, and how far back did your spying activities go and how long had I known you and where were you right now and when did I expect to see you again and they won't press any charges against me if I just give you up and help them arrest you and put you behind bars for a freakin' long time."

Palmer interrupted. "Are they there now?'

"NO!" Andi screamed. "But I'm here at work still shaking and Dominigo says I can go home early but we need the money so I'm staying here and there's tons of people coming in the door and I'm sitting on the toilet seat waiting until I freakin' compose myself so I can go out there and take their orders and get their drinks and act like I'm having fun so I can get a bigger tip and you're on the phone worrying about yourself and you don't care about the situation I'm in right now and you could care less that I'm stressed and developing a freakin' cold sore on my lip and my whole life is falling apart."

Palmer cringed. "Okay, okay, I hear you, I hear you. I'm in the cab. I'm about a block away. Can I come in the back door at the Plum Puddin' and talk with you, huh? Would that be good? I can be there in one minute. Will that help?"

"Help? Help? No that won't be any help. Those guys are probably hanging around looking for you. Shit, they know where we live. They've been watching us. They showed me photos they took through our windows and you're in the photos and I'm half nude and you're touching my body and they've got it all on film and they said they don't care if I cooperate or not, they're gonna take us both down and, no, they won't kill us but we could get put in a military prison or something and sent somewhere to be tortured until they find out everything we know."

"Jesus," Palmer whispered. "Okay. What should I do? I can't go home. This cabbie can take me out to Bonaventure. I'll go back there and hide. Anyway, my dad's gonna meet me out there at 8 pm. He could get me outta Savannah. Then maybe the Feds would stop bothering you. I could go back to Chapel Hill or maybe back to Sedalia with my Dad. Things will work out. Wadda ya think?"

Andi was sobbing, "I don't know. I don't really know. I hate being watched every single second and I hate being threatened and I hate working here and I should have stayed at my PT job in Chapel Hill and I had everything I wanted except you and now I can't have you anyways and you're so mixed up you don't even know how serious all this stuff is and maybe you shoulda just died in the Haw River."

14

Bitch's Brew

Heavy stuff to think about, and Morel craved a good dark beer. The cabbie dropped him off in front of the Moon River Brewery on Bay Street, promised he'd come and get him at 7:45.

Inside, the dark wood and dim lights took some time to get adjusted to, and Palmer walked slowly toward the bar.

Sitting at the end of the curved bar, he ordered his favorite, "Captain's Porter", and took a deep breath. He felt much safer here than on the streets, the hot, bright sun exposing him to danger on the sidewalk.

The beer was cold as he sipped and his eyes accustomed themselves to the surroundings. The dinner crowd had yet to arrive, only a few people at the tables and one old man sitting at the bar at the other end, his chair turned slightly like he was planning to leave.

What the fuck? Is this some goddam ghost? Palmer was startled by the man, so thin now, so somehow crooked, his head bent lower than he remembered.

He stood up quickly, grabbed his beer and moved fast down the length of the bar. "Dad, dad, I can't believe it," he said, his left hand resting on James Morel's right shoulder.

That familiar lopsided smile puckered up at Palmer and he gave Palmer's hand a squeeze. "Sit down, Palmer. Take a load off. It's like you woulda missed me. I was about to go."

Palmer moved abruptly. "Oops, sorry dad. Spilled some good beer on your shirt." He sat next to his dad, a big smile on his face.

James Morel checked his shirt, and then felt his pocket for the gun. Not much beer spilled, no pollution on his baby pistol.

Palmer broke the ice, "Hey, how's mom?"

"Doin' good. She's got that high blood pressure, you know. Worrying 'bout you don't help none."

Both Morels turned around to the bar, placing their feet on the rungs exactly the same way, cocking ther heads to size each other up in the same old way, running their left hands over their hair in exactly the same way. "God dammit, Palmer, what the hell you doin' down here in Savannah? Don't you know you'd be a lot better off back in Sedalia?"

"You're right, dad, you're right, but things happen."

"Did you read all that JFK stuff I sent you?"

"Most of it. I don't see the relevance to my situation."

James Morel smiled crookedly, "That's just it. You don't. But listen to me. It's the same thing. The military's using you. Wanted to kill you. Then you'd by their scapegoat."

Palmer shook his head, "For what? I don't think so. Mistaken identity maybe. But I'm not some important JFK guy, am I?"

"No, son. But you might be an Oswald. A patsy."

Palmer shook his head. "No. A patsy for what? I don't see that."

"Of course not, You think Oswald knew he was being set up? Not until they arrested him. You know I did some secret stuff like this after Nam?"

"Yeah, yeah. But that's over now, isn't it?"

James Morel smiled at his son. "It's never over."

"You mean you're still on the payroll?

His father nodded. "Maybe. And I know you're vulnerable for some shit to happen. Are you limping? Makes it harder for you to get away from any shit storm."

Palmer showed his right leg, "Yeah, got my calf punctured in the river, some passing tree branch. Toughest part's my shoulder. Got shot through and through. Can't lift it much yet but it's healing. I'm not really supposed to move around much."

"Let me see."

"See what?"

"Your shoulder."

Palmer turned his back to his dad and raised his shirt a little. "See it came in from the front at a high angle. Existed there under my shoulder blade. The scar's still healing, still a bit red."

His dad traced the scar with his thumb. "You're lucky to be alive, son."

Palmer nodded. "The river was real tough on me, but I stayed conscious and got thrown up on the shore there near the old Bynum bridge near Pittsboro. Friend helped me out, took me to the hospital."

"How long has it been now."

"About two months. My girl, Andi, has been bringing me back fom the dead. Good therapist. The best."

His dad grunted, "Yes, but you don't have to sleep with your therapist, you know. And, by the way. Watch out for that bitch. She might be setting you up."

***

Brianna kept knocking at the restaurant's bathroom door until Andi finally opened it up. "Watcha doin' in here, bitch? We're busy as hell. I need help and you're in here like some nut case. Get out of there I need to pee." And Brianna grabbed Andi's arm and flipped her out the doorway like some discarded cigarette butt.

And, as Andi returned to her station, she saw the freakin' Feds were back, camped out near the cold fireplace by the bar, sitting in those soft, too-short arm chairs, looking at their menus, giving her odd, twisted smiles as if they were torturing her on purpose.

"Bring me the flounder and some coffee," ordered the balding, chunky guy named Gene. They way he ordered seemed like a sneer, a threat and a sneeze all at the same time.

His buddy Stuart was more polite, the good cop, a little too sweet for a tall geeky-looking guy with a pale white face and thinning blond hair. "I'd like the pork shank, please. Some sweet tea. And a house salad. Thanks."

Andi turned to go, but Gene interrupted. "Aren't you gonna say anything, An—dray--a? We're customers, you know. Don't you want to smile and say you'll be right back with our drinks?"

Andi hurried away, her right arm raised, her fist waving her middle finger in the air. The Feds only laughed louder.

Returning from the restroom, punky Brianna saw the whole episode and blocked Andi's path as she tried to order the drinks from Domingo at the bar. "What are you fucking doing? Those are customers.
You can't give them the bird. The boss is gonna get an earful when I can talk to him, you phony bitch."

Andi ignored her, got Domingo's attention and placed the order. Then, she whipped around carrying an empty tray and caught the back of Brianna's head a glancing blow.

Immediately, Brianna reacted, grabbing the nap of hair at Andi's neck and pulling hard until Andi fell backwards onto the floor, the tray flew through the air and clattered against the wall, all the customers applauding like they did whenever someone dropped a load of dirty dishes.

Andi pounced up quickly, retrieved the tray and, as she passed Brianna gloating in the aisle, she pushed forward on her left leg and using her right foot kicked Brianna hard in the shin.

***

Joey planned his evening to be culminated in a sexual escapade involving Palmer Morel's girl friend, Andrea.

First, he called Domingo at the Plum Puddin'. He'd find some way to get Morel away from his townhome tonight, leaving Andi alone.

"Hey, change of plans, D. Got enuff pictures. Don't need you tonight. The Feds loved those nude pics I got yesterday. So, won't need more. I might need you for some strong arm involving a non-pay over on Tybee. You up for that in a day or two?"

Domingo took the call at the bar but moved outside. He walked to the middle of the square, listening to Joey back off the night's action. Good, he could let Andi leave early, let her escape from Brianna's harassment for a bit. "Yeah, I can help you. When? Saturday afternoon?"

Joey nodded, "Yeah, some guy in a rental on the beach. Still owes me some money from a bet on the U.S. Tennis Open. Fuckin' jerk. It won't take long. You hold 'em, I'll belt him."

"Uh, okay, you pick me up?"

"Yep, side entrance at the Plum Puddin' around 1 pm."

"Okay, see you Saturday then."

Joey clicked off and looked around the topless bar, not much action yet. The new girl looked young, but yet she looked experienced, with big naturals, a casual way of dancing, the locked-on-bored look of some runway models. She was one big turn-on. He hoped she was legal.

He watched her strip in front of a tiny audience of two old senior citizens wearing farmer joe outfits. Very slow evening. No tourists. No big spenders yet. The 9 pm show would bring them in, though, after their golf matches ended, their big dinners swallowed and a few drinks gulped out at Hilton Head Island.

He reached under the bar and popped two pills with a beer chaser. Then he sauntered back to the girls' dressing room, stopping at the stage to stuff a buck in the new girl's bikini bottom.

The dressing room was filling up with the girls from the Savannah Arts College, S.A.C. for short. Girls far away from home, artistic girls, painters, sculptors, a few actresses with great singing voices, all of them needing money and a little excitement. All of them lovin' to push the envelope a bit.

"Hi, Joey," a few of them called out, their lockers open, some of them sitting on the benches in front sort of like a football halftime scene.

"Hiya, things goin' good for yah? Looking to make some big bucks tonight?" He walked between them, touching them, caressing them like he owned all of them, which he did.

"Yeah, yeah, for sure," they echoed, each of them slipping out of their short-shorts, their T-shirts advertising a Mexican beer or a local beach, their long hair flowing toward the floor as they bent over to put on their costumes, their bare flesh working on Joey's psyche.

God, he loved women, and getting to Palmer's woman in a couple of hours was gonna be heaven. First, he'd go to the Lucas Theater as planned. Sign up a couple of the dancers who auditioned from the S.A.C musical troupe. Beautiful new topless young women. He loved it.

Then, he'd hang around a bit. Watch part of the musical review. Then, leave at intermission. Drive the three blocks to Morel's place across from the cemetery. Cause a disturbance out front. Sneak in through the back alley door, and....

15

Break-Up

"Palmer, Palm, can you come and get me. Domingo let me off early. I need to get out of here."

Morel listened, still sitting at the Moon River bar, talking to his dad. "Sure, sure, I 've got someone here at the bar you need to meet."

"For God's sake, Palm. This isn't a social meet-up. Come and get me now. Get us a cab or whatever. The Feds were here and I'm shaking like crazy. I can't take this."

"Okay, okay, I'll be right over. Where will you be?"

"I'll check out my tips, then go across the street to Reynolds Square. There's some benches near my car, I think. But hurry up and I don't want to meet any of your freakin' drinking buddies."

After she clicked off, Palmer turned to his dad. "See. I told you. She still needs me. Wants me to come get her. I'm sort of relieved."

"Humpf, sounded like she was ordering you around. I could hear her voice way over here. What are you gonna do about the Feds? Won't they be watching, plotting?"

"Maybe, but shit, dad, you worry too much. You have your car nearby, right? You go get it. I'll hide in here, meet you outside when you pull up. The Plum Puddin' is just two blocks away. We'll park on the other side of the square, then Andi can get in with us. She can leave her car there over night. No problem."

They both scuffed their chairs away from the bar, Palmer left a ten dollar tip, and they went near the door. "I'll stay here till you park. It's a red Buick, right?"

James Morel was half out the doorway, "Yes, it's just a short walk down the street. Five minutes tops. Where we gonna go after we get Andi?"

Palmer hesitated, "Well, if the Feds are still outside the Plum Puddin', we can go back to our home, get some stuff, lock up, fool the Feds, and sneak out the back and go stay at Bonaventure again."

Mr. Morel was surprised, "Back out to that cemetery? How in hell can you be comfortable out there? That's not a good hiding place."

Palmer laughed at that, "Oh, yes, it is. Kept me safe and unseen for awhile."

But James Morel knew better. "You can never shake the Feds."

***

The drama director for "Remembering the Fifties," Colin Whitaker, could be a real asshole if anyone challenged his choices, his dramatic interpretations or his integrity. And the freakin' mobster who was always hanging around the Lucas Theater talking to his female cast members was way up there on his cringe list.

Joey "Spider" Lingua was a touchy-feely mobster, always approaching women with his hands, always touching them, caressing their clothes, reaching for their hair to straighten a contrary wisp. The guy gave Colin the creeps, but the girls seemed to eat that stuff up. "Oh, he's Italian," he heard one of the girls from the chorus blurt out, as if Italian was something special.

Colin had checked the guy out on the web and he was a convicted petty crook, the so-called owner of a strip joint across the river in South Carolina and one of the owners of Drayton Trolleys, supposedly supervising the "Ghastly Ghosts" trolleys throughout the historic district.

And here he was, right before curtain time, schmoozing with Colin's girls, his leading lady, his chorus line. This would have to stop. His meddling was causing a lack of attention, a lack of professionalism, and Colin had had enough.

"You. Yes, you, the guy in the tight white pants. Get over here."

Joey turned around, his arm still on the shoulder of Jilly Martin, lead singer and gorgeous blonde,.

Joey forced his smile, let go of Jilly for the moment and took one step toward Colin. "Wadda ya want, fruitcake?"

***

After the little Plum Puddin' rumble, the two federal officers had not had a chance to place their dessert orders. In fact, they hadn't seen their waitress, Andrea, for the last ten minutes since her noisy altercation involving the other waitress. Had she been too upset to continue? Was she hurt? Was she still angry with them for showing up at her work place?

Gene nodded his head toward the bar. "Stuart, go ask the bartender to send another waitress over here. Ask him what happened to Andrea."

The lanky FBI agent grumbled, but uncrumpled his long legs, pushing up from the low-slung chair with his arms. He ambled to the bar, waited while Domingo finished a drink order, and then made his request. "Hey, bartender. We need some dessert over at our table. Where's our waitress?"

Domingo answered, "She went home early. I'll get Brianna over there to help you."

"Whatsa matter with the other one? Is she sick?"

"No, no, nothing like that. She wanted to get off early. She's been working long hours. She's tired. Hey, Brianna. Take care of these gentlemen, will you?"

Still grumpy, Brianna gave Domingo some attitude but walked over to the Feds' table. "What can I do for ya?"

Gene took a moment, sized her up. Maybe she might be the type to share some off-the-cuff information. "Yeah, yeah. We'd like desserts. Bring us some ice cream, okay?"

"Fine, I'll bring them out." Brianna turned to leave but Gene called her back.

"Hey, what's up with the other waitress. She got an attitude. She don't like you or what?"

Brianna gave her bitter smile. "No, we don't get along." She raised her leg. "Look at this freakin' bruise. She kicked me."

"You gonna press charges?"

"What? No, no. We just don't get along. It's okay. She says she's under a lot of stress. She and her boy friend are gonna leave Savannah, go back to Carolina. She doesn't like it here."

Gene nodded, "I see. When's she leaving?"

Brianna looked peeved, "Look, you want your desserts tonight or not?"

"Just asking."

"She's going back to Chapel Hill tonight. Gave notice to Domingo a minute ago. Good riddance is what I say."

Gene looked at Stuart, then pulled out his cell phone. Texting, he wrote, *You can't drop out. Carry out your assignment.* Then he sent the text to Andi's phone.

***

Cat Gallaher couldn't believe the phone call she got. With lightning flashing all around and the constant crash of big boomers from the Carolina thunderstorm, she wondered how her phone stayed connected. And shouldn't she put the phone down during a storm or was that dangerous only with land lines?

But there it was. Andrea's disembodied voice explaining her plan, her return to Chapel Hill, the horror of being watched by the Feds all the time in Savannah. So, could she come to Deerington Village and stay with Cat for awhile? Could she pay something to help with the rent until she could get her PT job back again? And she knew that the Palmer Morel thing might get between them, but she had no one else to go to now? Please, Cat, can't you help? She would be leaving immediately and would arrive in Deerington in six hours. Would that be okay?

Cat had said yes, fine. You can stay. But now it was just after eight pm, the storm's booming noise was moving east, and TJ was cuddled beside her on the couch, very afraid of the storm and too wound up to go to bed yet.

Six hours. If she explained it all to Morel and if she had the guts to pack up and leave by nine pm, Andrea could be knocking on Cat's door by three am. Great! The damn middle-of-the-night and she'd have an un-needed guest, perhaps a bigger problem from the Feds and another distraction for TJ's little damaged psyche. Shit!

But what else could she do? She was actually bouyantly happy inside. Andrea was leaving Palmer. Hurrah!

***

As soon as James Morel pulled his big red car behind Andi's little Kia near Reynolds Square, Andi put away her phone and rushed across the street opening the back door to get in. "Palmer, I'm done with this. I'm going back to Chapel Hill."

She climbed into the car and scootched over to sit in the back seat directly behind Palmer who was sitting in the front passenger seat.

"What? Did something happen, Andi? Andi, when did you decide this?"

"Listen, I'm going. I don't need to talk. I don't need any advice. Just take me over to get my stuff and then bring me back here to my car, Palmer. I can't take this shit any more."

Palmer's dad listened silently, the engine running quietly, the hiss of Savannah's nightly insects creating a backdrop of tension like in a horror movie. He thought, *She can't desert the plan.*

Finally, Palmer tried again. "Andi, this here's my dad. Do you want to meet him?"

Andi reacted only with her eyes, scanning from Palmer to the man at the steering wheel, an elderly man slowly turning around, his right hand outstretched. "Pleased to meet ya, Andi."

She took his hand and sighed, "Hi."

After an awkward pause, Palmer said, "Okay, dad. Go around the square and then go south past the Lucas Theater. Our home is about three blocks away down Abercorn."

Andi leaned back against her seat, refusing to hold Palmer's hand as Mr. Morel moved carefully around the narrow square, then headed slowly south.

In a few minutes, he parked across the street from their townhome on Oglethorpe across from Colonial Cemetery. "If you guys need to talk, I can drop you off and then come back in a half hour or so, or I could just sit in the car when you go inside."

No one moved to get out. Palmer again turned around to establish eye contact with Andi, but she was looking out the window into the darkening depths of the cemetery.

"I'm going back to Carolina," she whispered.

16

Close Up

The Lucas Theater audience hushed to a whisper as the curtain went up for the "Remembering the Fifties" and the five dancing gals skipped on stage dressed in their pink short skirts, sparkly white blouses and black/white saddle shoes. The five male dancers looked cool as they moved with their bright white slacks, light pink polo shirts and white bucks.

The only discordant note was the Italian who pushed Colin headfirst into a corner after the opening curtain. "Listen, you little twit. I'll do anything I want here. Mind your own fuckin' choreography. Leave the girls to me."

Colin was gasping for breath, Joey's thumbs pushing against his Adam's apple. Finally, he croaked an "Okay," and a smirking Joey released him. Both glared at each other a moment.

Then Joey laughed. "Let's keep it light, Mr. Twit. There's enough fun for all of us backstage. Relax. It's all over"

Joey smiled again and watched the dance routine onstage. The little orchestra was knocking out some old-time rock and roll, the audience of retirees was clapping to "Hound Dog," and the cute dancers were whirling.

But Colin quickly left the scene of the attack, hurrying back to his dressing room, grabbing a bottle of water and sitting down in front of the mirror, seeing the red marks on his neck. *Nothing is over*, he said to himself. *Nothing is ever over.*

Taking out his cell phone, he hit 9-1-1. He sipped from the bottle carefully until the Dispatcher answered. "Your emergency?"

"I'm at the Lucas Theater, backstage. I've just been attacked," he rasped.

"Sir, speak up. You say you've been attacked?"

"Yes, ma'am. And the bastard is still in the theater."

***

It was merely act of courtesy that the Savannah police sergeant called the local office of the FBI to report an altercation involving one of the Fed's favorites, mob member Joey Laguna.   For many years the Feds used Joey for various jobs: photographer, drug spy, street gang newsie, and pimp for some of their own surreptitious, sexual needs. Joey had a supply of young, gorgeous women and the Feds and the local PD liked to tap into them for some afternoons of bliss in their squad cars or in the evenings at some Tybee Island motels.

FBI Agent Gene and his buddy Stuart finished their desserts and walked slowly to their car outside the Plum Puddin'. Their boy Joey was causing a ruckus over at the Lucas Theater and they were in no real hurry to bail him out. The Savannah blues would handle him for awhile. Joey always needed a lesson it seemed, and being forced to sit in a patrol car would do him some good.

But, Stuart thought about the chance for sexual adventure. *God, the evening is lovely, a warm southwest breeze moving the low-hanging moss, a smell of something like lavender in the air and the chance for some southern-college-girl-loving a real possibility. We'd get Joey off the hook, and he'd be real happy to send a few girls to ouir downtown hotel at Ellis Square on West Bay later on. Good times.*

***

Understanding was something James "Pops" Morel took for granted. A bookish man with a talent for athletics and woodworking, he'd spent a good bit of his time in gyms, basements and garages, both working and reading, solving problems, keeping his past military life a secret.

His basement in Sedalia was not cut too deep so that the southern windows still revealed his backyard full of tiger lilies, blackbirds and the tall yuccas his wife loved. He could sit there awhile and read, the summer sun hot on his back if he turned the swivel chair around so he faced the old, converted coal furnace. This is where he had done his JFK reading, where he had written to his congressmen, trying to understand assassination and its place in America's politics, feeling guilty about the special operations he had carried out himself in Dallas.

Now he sat in his car this evening in Savannah, his son inside his townhome with his girl, Andi, each of them confused about the suddenness of a goodbye, a decision upsetting his son more than anything his father could remember.

As he struggled to understand, he tried to get a handle on the sexual tension that had developed in his son's relationship with this phyical therapist. Massages, tenderness, love. All a mistake Andi knew better. She had a job to do, that's all James knew. And, if she didn't cxarry it out, he would take care of her.

He saw her anger, her determination to get back to Chapel Hill. She must have snapped. She was walking out on her special ops task.Just now, his son had followed her passionately into their rental home, an older brick townhome, connected to a poet's old home. But his son was following death.

Conrad Aiken, as a kid, must have viewed the cemetery across the way, just as James Morel did now. The poet must have sounded out some horrifying words about the dead and dying, after experiencing the tragic deaths of his parents. Maybe he had stumbled upon the words that celebrated love and its death, just the same type of words that Palmer might be using inside his home now as he tried to get Andi to stay with him. But Palmer just didn't know. He was out of his depth.

Her resolution seemed so strong, to travel back up highway 95 toward Raleigh, Durham, and Chapel Hill; however, James Morel knew the real situation. This woman was a government operative. His own task was clear.

He tried to catch sight of the couple inside, looking through the windows, but he could see nothing through the dark, drawn shades.

Andi had said she'd be down soon, with her things, and then James would drive her back to her car. And she would commence immediately with her ride back highway 95 to Raleigh, Durham and Chapel Hill, hoping to get there by three a.m. when she would meet

Palmer's former girl, the stripper Cat Gallaher, and stay in her apartment in Deerington with Palmer's little son, TJ.

He could not understand Palmer's loss of love for Cat, nor his new love of this physical therapist, Andi, who seemed so lost herself. He couldn't understand the violent attack on his son a few months ago that almost killed him. Because Palmer could not think of what he had done to enrage the government, James could not understand why the FBI was still interested in catching Palmer or perhaps killing Palmer. Instead, he thought the Feds were setting him up.

Of course, James was old, confused at times now, not completely able to develop an ingenius plan to keep his son and grandson safe. He pulled out his little .25 baby gun, the one he thought might help protect his son from these forces trying to destroy him. But he was in conflict. He'd have to take out Andi first. In his fear he thought he understood the power of a gun to improve a situation growing in suspicion and danger. But improvement for whom? His son was romantically involved with the target.

He began to understand that his trip from Sedalia was growing into tragedy. He found some strength and security found in his small calibre weapon. He liked the way the gun felt in his hand. And, he understood that, if he had to, he would use it.

***

Andi tried to make Palmer see her point of view. She had a good life before she met him. Now she must leave. Had to. She could not help him any more. His physical therapy was almost over anyway, wasn't it?. He was in good shape, wasn't he? Her professional job was done, wasn't it?

Why had she ignored her professional standards for this man? Was he so special? Was she so lonely that she fell for his attention, his kindness, his light blue eyes? Now she was so ineffective she couldn't carry out her mission for the USA government. But she could not kill Palmer.

As she packed her two luggage bags, she kept shaking her head, no more, no more, no more. She turned to look at Palmer, emotionally upset on the couch, following her movements through the townhome, over to the bedroom, back to the kitchen, to the bookshelf, picking out the three books she had brought with her. But they had stayed unopened, untouched, throughout her time in Savannah.

There. She was finished. She sat down hard on the largest bag, pushed it down until the latches snapped shut on the books. She smiled at Morel. The action of packing, of taking charge again, left her feeling happy, optimistic.

"I'm ready now, Palmer."

***

"Godammit," Joey yelled from the backseat of the patrol car toward Officer C. T. Childress who was sitting on the curb, waiting for the Feds to show up at the scene. The Lucas Theater lights brightened the street and Childress was practicing his patience as Joey kept yelling at him.

"Don't you know who I am? You think you can shove me inside your fuckin' car and think I won't do something? I know those dancers. I know them well, and they like me. Like me! Why did you believe that Colin fruitcake when he called 911? He's nothing, nothing. I'm not a molester. I'm not a rapist."

Childress pushed his big body up from the curb and walked to the patrol car's open backseat window. "Look, Joey. I know the situation here. We called your buddies in the government. They'll handle this little incident quickly. You know that. Why are you being such a big weenie tonight?"

Joey shook his head. Looked at his watch. "I'll tell you why. I've got an important meeting at 10 p.m. and I'm gonna be late because you boys believed some little fruit fly. That's it. That's the whole deal right there."

Childress smiled as a big black car pulled up in front of the theater. "Here's your friends now. And, look. It's only 9:30. You can make that so-called big meeting after all."

17

Zippo

What was keeping Palmer and Andi? It had been half an hour at least and the old Vet's leg muscles were tightening up. The long drive from Raleigh had caused his body to stiffen and he needed to get out of the car and walk around.

He slowly moved his legs, got out, put his gun in his belt holster and headed for the Colonial cemetery gate. A good walk around the unspeaking dead might clear his brain as he got his blood flowing through his legs. Jesus, it was hard getting old!

His wife would probably be bugging him from back in Sedalia soon Calling Palmer or something. She didn't like James meddling in other people's lives, taking secret trips to do god knows what, and she thought coming down to Savnnah might put Palmer in harm's way, but, shit, Palmer was in trouble anyway. If he could get Palmer to Bonaventure Cemtery, and do the job on Andi, his trip would be worth it.

He took the entire path once around Colonial, watching his car to see if his son had come out of the townhouse, but nothing was going on.

So, he went back to his car and sat on the hood, but his legs cramped up again, Shit, he'd have to go inside and get them out here. Andi wanted to get back to Chapel Hill by three a.m. They'd better get going. He had no idea what project she had failed to do, but she evidently knew too much to live. He'd pretend to drive her to her car and take care of her somewhere in some alley in Savannah. Make it look like a robbery. Then, get back to his son. Talk some sense to him.

Business-like now, he walked across Oglethorpe and started up the stairs, but he heard a car traveling around the block and he waited to watch it pass by. *Was it the Feds?* Nope, just some daek-haired guy going by real slow, looking up at Palmer's home. *Who the fuck is he?*

***

It was time for her 10 p.m. cigarette break and punked-up waitress, Brianna Taylor, grabbed her trendy Capri cigarettes, her phone and her Zippo "Ozzy Osbourne" lighter, raced out into the warm night and into Reynolds Square where she could puff away and make some prank calls.

She loved her Zippo. She had picked it up at the Zippo Museum in Bradford, Pennsylvania. As she smoked, she turned the Zippo in her hand, looking at all its red and black details. Ozzy. What an old nasty guy! Not really too sexy now, but she loved his attitude and stone-cold death images.

She hoped her nemesis, the evil Andi Pandi, might have been forced out of the Plum Puddin' for good; if not, she'd invade her space with a little trickery to get her out. Since Brianna had a secretive privacy phone listing, with no return phone number, she could prank call anyone with impunity. And often did.

Andi Pandi could never prove who was calling her, and she could give the little physical therapy brat some real physical threats to hurt her, direct the threats of pain at the DPT's own prissy legs and arms.

The light menthol hit Brianna's lungs and she got a bit of a buzz. She loved these cool, thin cigs, stylish and mild. She took out Domingo's note with Andi's number and clicked it into her phone with her middle thumb. She got ready to text and waited till she finished her cigarette. Wouldn't Andi be surprised?

***

James Morel got antsy, very impatient. He had watched the car drive by again, and the guy looked like some mafia-type or hit man, a little like Jack Ruby in the JFK murder, the guy who shot Oswald. Pops needed to act. Maybe the guy was after Palmer? Who knew with these government conspiracists? James was multi-tasking, now protecting his son and soon carrying out a hit of his own.

He coninued up the stairs and tried the door. Open. Well, that was just plain stupid. Leaving the door open when the Feds and god-knows-who-else is looking for you. Once inside, James locked the door and pulled the bolt too. Couldn't be too safe.

"Palmer? Andi," his shouts echoed into the back bedroom.

"Pops? Why'd you come inside? We were just coming out?" Palmer said, leading Andi by the hand down the hallway, the old, bare, wood floor adding to the echo of his words.

James was confused. "You guys make up, or what? She still going back to Chapel Hill, need me to drive her to her car?"

Then a cell phone rang. Andi picked through her purse and picked up her new phone; her ring tone was from a song by Depeche Mode, "Enjoy the Silence."

Andi listened to the voice. No identification, just an extended rant, a long threat of violence, vocalized by some crazed, gutteral-voiced woman, her voice like an echo of a witch. Andi's eyes grew wider and wider. She used her right hand and brushed her hair off her neck. Creepy.

Andrea. Andrea. Don't go out. I can see you. Don't go out. I'm waiting for you. All your babies will be dead. Dead. Dead. Dead.

Then, Andi screamed.

***

It's hard at night to detect the backdoors of the townhomes along Oglethorpe, even in the daylight. The fenced backdoors are not numbered, being connected to large, elaborate gardens full of flowers, miniature trees, expensive lawn equipment, elaborate barbecuing areas and, at times, deep shade.

As Joey carefully walked down the alleyway, he couldn't remember which townhome was Andi's. He was still frustrated by the entire Lucas Theater debacle, just thankful that the Feds acted quickly and freed him. These symbiotic government contacts were always fruitful to him and the mob.

Stopping under the only dimly-lit-yellow streetlight in the alley, he took a deep breath. He usually got too excited on these sexual adventures, and tonight his heart was racing. He'd had just one beer, chugged it down in the car to calm himself. But the alcohol had no positive effect. He wanted Andi, but could not get into the mood, too frustrated by anger now, lost in the alley of gardens, unable to find the right house.

Shit, he'd have to go around to the front and count the doorways so he could return to the alley with the correct number of homes. He turned and started to jog back to the street, when a piercing shriek penetrated his brain. *What the hell was that?*

One loud scream, then silence. No shouts. No doors opening. No one on the streets. No sirens. Waiting a minute more, he then continued back to Oglethorpe, counted all the townhomes until he came to the seventh home, Andi's.

He whirled around, more violent, more eager, planning how he'd get inside, how he'd get to Andi, how he'd tie her up. Breathing heavily, he ran down the alley, counting off the backdoors, 1-2-3-4-5-6-7.

Okay, now to get in.

※※※

"Just relax, Dad," Palmer explained after Andi's scream. "The call might be no one we know. It was a message from a private caller. Could be a wrong number."

"But it was a threat? Right? Not just some wrong number?" James Morel role-played. "Shouldn't we call the police?"

"Dad, Dad. No. We can't and you know why. We can't reveal our location, nothing."

Andi remained seated in the rocker in the darkened living room, moving the chair slowly, her head resting on her right hand, searching for composure.

Finally, "I think I need to go. Take me to my car. I'm okay now. Really. Let's just do this now. I don't want to be late. Cat's waiting for me."

Palmer said, "No way are you ready, Andi. No way. It's a long ride. Give Cat a call. Tell her you'll stay here until morning. Get a fresh start. She'll understand."

But Palmer's Dad still pretended, his hand on the .25 baby in its holster. "She's going? I thought you were back together. I mean, it seemed like it. You know, I saw you holding hands. That's a good sign, isn't it?"

Then the phone rang again, and again. Andi's ring-tone repeating...*Enjoy the silence, Enjoy the silence!*

Andi jumped up. "What should I do?" She started to grab the phone as it lit up on the table.

Palmer grabbed her tightly. "No, let it ring; don't answer. Let it roll over. Then we'll have the voice. We need that voice for identification. Let it ring."

Depeche Mode, Depeche Mode, Depeche Mode, five more times. Then the ring tone stopped.

Mr. Morel broke the silence. "They must have our location. You said that photographer knows our location. The Feds know our location. Everybody knows our location. Who are we hiding from if they all know our location? Isn't Andi leaving now? What?"

***

Once inside the garden, Joey still had to get inside Andi's home. Locating the correct key on the large key ring, Joey quietly slipped it into the back door lock, carefully balancing himself on the little porch. He knew how these old townhomes worked: just a little entranceway, then a few steps into the first-floor living area. Old doors. Olds locks. He used plastic as the key. The lock was open. He pushed the old door with the little doggie entrance below; it opened silently.

Stepping inside, using both hands, he swung the door slowly back in its place. It clicked shut. Looking around, he had enough dim light to get his bearings. Moving past the refrigerator, the sink, the counter, he peered down the hall into the ornate dining room, the long table made of dark wood, the golden, octogonal chandelier, the fireplace, the large entrance to the living room facing the street, then another fireplace.

To his right was the staircase, the white railing, and next to it was the extensive wet bar. No one seemed to be down stairs. Where were they? He heard voices. He knew Morel was with Andi. He'd have to get him outside, maybe on an errand? But how?

Wait a minute, he thought. *They're coming down the stairs. Shit!*

Where could he hide? It was all so open. He retreated back to the dark kitchen, dropped his keys, accidentally kicking them against the wall, moved behind the table near the window, then hid himself under the table. *Goddam! This is the wrong place to hide.*

Joey was trapped.

18

Romance

TJ was such a pest! Cat knew kids could sense something in the air, but this behavior was beyond weird.

First, he piled up all his blocks, two hundred and five at last count, and organized them into the outline of a crazed bumblebee, similar to the ones at the entrance to Deerington Village.

Second, he used his little train tracks to encircle the bumblebee, allowing room for train bridges and train stoplights and train people.

Then, he raced off to his room, searching for something. She could hear him tearing open his boxes and opening drawers. What was it?

When he returned, Cat tried her best not to be astounded, but he had grabbed the 8 X 10 photo of his dad, Palmer, taken before the shooting at the Haw River. Palmer looked gigantic and athletic, his muscles popping out of his pec-displaying short T-shirt, the one photo that TJ loved the best.

He placed the photo among the bumblebee blocks so it looked like Palmer was riding the bumblebee on some desperate mission. What an imagination!

And as TJ played, he carried on a conversation with his dad, with the bumblebee and with his "Thomas the Train" toy set, moving trains here and there, allowing some trains to crash and crumple over.

So, he used the Palmer photo to swoop down on the "injured" trains, turn them over and start them on another journey through bumblebee-land. Palmer was saving the day like Superman!

Cat had not yet told TJ about the coming visit of the dreaded Andi, the mighty physical therapist, saviour of Palmer's health, and she couldn't tell him now, since TJ had to get to bed soon. No use getting him more excited. So, she waited and watched, giggling quietly each time TJ would blurt out, "Watch out, Mr. Bee. Dad's gon get you now!"

Cat looked at her watch. 10 p.m. Just five hours before Andi would arrive. She guessed they both better get some sleep. "Come on, Teeej. Time for nighty-night. Here, let me help you pick up your toys."

But TJ wouldn't allow it. "No, no. Leeb 'em there. Want show dad when he gets home."

***

"Andi, just lie down for awhile, over here in the living room. You, too, Pops. Snuggle down in a chair. There's plenty of time for Andi to leave. We can give Cat a call, say Andi will be late. No problem."

Andi had finally decompressed a bit from her rock-hard, big, emotional scene, having moved the fear from the telephone call back into the depths of her brain.

She also had lost some of her zip, her push to get out of Savannah. "Palm, Palm, okay. I'll rest a bit. Really. It's okay. Go out. Watch your goddam spooky trolley go by. I don't care. But, hey, before you go, come here and give me a kiss you big lug."

Morel brightened up. "You mean it?" He held Andi softly in his strong arms, his lips just brushing hers, wanting more of her, not wanting to leave.

"Are you really going to go away?"

Andi looked into those light-blue eyes. "I think so. I'll talk when you get back. Now go. Find out all about Savannah's ghosts. I'll nap."

Palmer spoke quietly to his dad, "Pops, you gonna be all right here. No problems?"

But his dad was already out, his head lolling, his gray hair mussed up a bit from his long day.

"Dad?"

Andi brought Palmer down to her level, kissing him again. "He's fine. Now leave us be. I'll look after your dad. But be back in a a couple of hours."

Palmer picked her up in his arms and gently set her down on the couch. "I'll be back for more, Sweets." He smiled walked to the front door and was gone.

***

Joey's body relaxed, but his brain was making computer noises, electricity zapping his synapses, sweat sizzling down his brow like a bad Elvis youtube video. So, Morel was gone to check out Joey's own ghost tour and ride the trolley? So, then, Joey was going on a tour to ride Morel's girl.

Joey liked that analogy. But he still waited. He figured he had two hours till Morel returned from the ghost tour. But the old man posed a problem: what if the old man did not stay asleep?

Joey figured he could drug the sleeping Andi quickly with the chloroform cotton gag he had all ready in his plastic bag of tricks along with his gun.

Plan: Get her upstairs. Tie her down to a bed.

But the old man was a problem. Where did he come from? Why was he here?

Using the slippery wooden floor to advantage, Joey slid his body away from the kitchen table and into the open hallway. If the dozing inhabitants looked up, he was still below their sight lines. He could slide noiselessly all the way to the dining room before he would hit the first rug. And he did that now, quickly, effortlessly.

He paused to listen. Easy breathing from Andi, her left leg hanging off the side of the couch. A rasping wheeze from the old man. Shit, if the old man awoke, he'd be easy to take down. Physical stamina and the element of surprise in Joey's favor. He didn't want to hurt the old man, but he would if he had to. Wouldn't take much. A choke hold. Out in seconds.

But he had to get ready. He pushed himself back into the kitchen, sliding the whole way. He took off his shoes, socks, shorts, T-shirt. He held onto his plastic bag. Grabbed a towel from the hook near the sink. Placed the towel under his butt. Moved across the floor like some nude acrobat.

He was so excited he could hear his own heartbeat.

***

Morel was smiling as he moved gracefully through the street, his heart full of joy and excitement. He had decided to jog slowly over to the trolley station. Test his recovering legs.

He knew you could get anywhere in downtown Savannah within minutes. What he'd do first was take a ride on the ghost trolley, "Ghastly Ghosts," check out the job of trolley barker, the job he'd be doing soon, and see what the ghost script might be like. He knew all these barkers were given the same script to memorize.

Only difference was the personality put into it. Some barkers would be more successful than others, made the tourists laugh or, better yet, get them spooked. Then, he might get a larger tip unless, of course, he maybe scared them so much they wanted off the trolley and didn't leave a tip.

But Morel was sure he could do the job. He'd had twenty years of giving tennis lessons, jollying up older women so they'd enjoy tennis more, breaking down the barriers of teenagers with a bad attitude, getting them to loosen up, have fun playing tennis.

And then earlier, he'd managed to get Andi laughing, quickly getting her nude and into the shower with him while his dad waited in the car, spending so much time teasing her breasts with soap the lather was so thick they looked like little, pointed, snow mountains, and then having sex with her right there in the warm shower, using his hands creatively, loving away all her fears about the Feds and her anger toward that antagonistic co-worker over at the Plum Puddln'.

After the sex, it felt like he and Andi were right back to the early days of their relationship, back as lovers and buddies who could do anything in the world. He was sure she would stay with him now. Only thing left to do was to call Cat, tell her Andi wasn't going back to Chapel Hill after all.

***

Parking on the other side of Colonial Cemetery and then walking a few blocks in the dark over to Morel's house on Oglethorpe wasn't Federal Agent Stuart Moon's idea of good police procedure.

First, someone could break into their car, steal their stuff. Second, in an emergency it would be hard for them to retrieve their weaponry or make a getaway, Third, it was night for god's sake and Savannah's sidewalks were notoriously bumpy, broken and bitchy. All he needed now was a misstep and he'd turn an ankle.

But he agreed with his partner, Gene Cooke, that Joey needed to be monitered. Joey had used the excuse tonight that he needed to go to a "meeting" at 10 o'clock, couldn't ride with them so they could find out more about his misadventure down at the Lucas Theater. Shit, everybody at headquarters knew that Joey was a serial rapist. He'd done this many times before. Hadn't they bailed him out three times in five years for such horrendous acts? Stuart even knew the guy's tactics.

Enter through a back door. Strip himself naked. Wait till the victim was asleep. Gag her and tie her up. Rape her doggy style. Escape out the back door and into his waiting car.

They had the victims' testimony. They had the rape kit tests, the DNA. They had Joey each time, but each time Joey had been released because of his "value" to our Feds. Personally, Stuart would have castrated the bastard after his first attack.

Reaching the front of Morel's home, Stuart asked Gene, "Shouldn't we go round back, stop the bastard before he gets inside?"

Gene sighed, "Probably not. He's no doubt active already. He's efficient, you know. It's been an hour since we let him go. He's got her tied up. If we went in now, there'd be a scene. Don't want to upset the boss by getting involved. You know, Joey don't hurt his victims. Just uses them. No. No. We'll just go back to the alley, wait, and then get him after he's done. He won't do anything too stupid. No harm, no foul.

Need a cigarette?"

19

Silence

Just don't do nothin' stupid, Joey said to himself, now that Andi and the old man were asleep in the living room. *Don't move too fast. Just go to her face, use the chloroform, hold it over her mouth and nose, get her up the stairs to the bedroom.*

It still stayed very awkward, the foot of the man's reclining chair close to the couch. Joey would have to lift Andy up and over the recliner without waking the old man. Bending over Andi, he could smell her clothing, her hair. Something like a fragrant aloe or soap, like after having taken a shower. A wonderful aroma. He was intoxicated now, nearly overcome by her beauty, her essence.

He placed his left hand near her shoulder, the chloroformed handerkerchief close to her nose, his right hand under her legs. Her thin summer robe fell open slightly, revealing her legs. He paused. She was gorgeous.

He began again, breathing hard now, a little nervous, shaking, hoping to cover her nose and mouth quickly, so her next breath would take in a huge amount of fumes.

But then a horrifying noise…a cellphone, ringing, ringing, a cellphone, where was it?

"*Violence….pain….pleasure….harm…in my arms…pain….pleasure…feelings…pain….violence.*"

Andi's ring tone blasted the silence. *Depeche mode. Depeche mode.* She awoke abruptly, clicked the phone, then saw Joey's face inches from her own.

Joey dropped his handkerchief, the old man sat upright in his chair.

There was a pause, then a familiar raspy voice spoke from the phone: *All your pretty ones will be dead. All. You won't survive. You won't survive. Your world will end. You'll go away. Go away and never come back.*

And Andi shrieked, her shrill scream rising, rising, her face reddening and her fear growing, growing.

And the old man was fully, searched his pockets, then his holster. He found his baby. He stretched his arm straight toward Joey and Andi, and he pulled the trigger.

Instantly, blood from Andi's head splattered Joey's face, dripped from his lips.

Joey spun away from Andi, rolled to the floor, dropping his handkerchief, reaching for his gun inside the plastic bag, and he found the trigger, firing wildly at the old man,

But the old man somehow stood up, firing his weapon till it was empty.

And there was no movement on the couch. There was no motion on the floor.

The old man collapsed backwards onto the recliner, his flannel shirt oozing red.

***

Cost him twenty-five bucks, but leaning back into his seat Morel was happy to be on the ghost trolley, heading east toward a late visit to the sailors' ghosts at the old Pirate's House. He hoped Andi was comfortable back home. She was just so stressed. He felt concerned about her health, but he really needed her here with him. He couldn't picture his life without her.

Not too many tourists were on board, but sitting at the back he could watch them as they reacted to the older barker's ghost spiel as he talked into the microphone:

"...and some waitresses have seen faces reflected off the mirrors, but when they turned to look, no one was there. Guests have heard ominous heavy breathing in the hallways, and in the basement Blackbeard's visage hangs on a wall, presaging sounds of ancient screams of fear..."

Morel liked the script. Could use some more humor, though. He'd have to find some good stories to add. Maybe some tourist jokes, a few true stories of modern pirates, some more details of ghostly rape and pillage.

The ride in the back of the trolley proved to be a bit bumpy, but his seat offered him a good view of Bay Street and the hill down to the river. It was a warm night, perfect for romantic escapades, jazz from the bars and restaurants adding a pleasant ambiance for any visitor. Moon River, Churchill's. Tourists getting a late night snack.

The trolley worked its way carefully through the riverfront. The cobblestones added an extra level of bumps for his back to endure, but soon the trolley climbed the hill to East Bay.

Just past the river entertainment centers, the trolley turned into the small parking lot and the tourists filed outside for the short walk to the front door of the supposedly ghost-filled Pirate House. Morel hopped down the exit last, feeling the warm breeze and excited about seeing the inside of the famed pirate den.

In the background of the street sounds, he heard sirens, lots of them, zooming down the streets a few blocks away. Something's happening. A fire? A car wreck? A wild car chase through the narrow streets?

He stopped a tourist who was using ear buds to add music to his evening. "Hey, buddy. Hear those sirens?"

The bearded man in his forties took out his ear buds and smiled, saying," What? Sorry. Couldn't hear you. Listening to some older Depeche Mode. Probably had the volume up too high. What'd you say, again?"

Morel could hear the song "Enjoy the Silence" through the man's ear buds.

***

The waitress was seated on the bathroom toilet, listening hard, her cigarette burning itself down to a nub. She strained to hear her cell phone over the piano music down the hall. She wasn't supposed to smoke in the restroom, but she needed to get up the nerve to harass Andi again, and the nicotine worked.

When she had almost finished making her pseudo-scary message to Andi on the phone, she heard Andi scream, then came loud popping noises: gunshots, first two quick ones - - -pop - - -pop - - -then a pause - - -and then three louder shots - - - boom---boom--- boom - - - then a quick volley of five more smaller calibre - - - pop - - -pop - - -pop - - -pop - - - pop - - - pop……..then silence.

Listening for more, her heart beating wildly, she waited, then clicked off. Immediately, there was loud knocking on the restroom door. "Brianna, Brianna. Are you smoking in there? It's against the rules. Get out here…now."

Domingo was sure pissed off. So, she stood up, threw the cigarette into the toilet and flushed it down. She looked in the mirror, straightened her uniform, pushed her hair back with her hand and opened the door.

"What? I'm not smoking, but some customer was before I got in. You can still smell it. See?"

Domingo was not fooled. "Listen, I've warned you before. Go outside to smoke. Go over to the square. I'm not breaking any laws for you. Now, get out here. You're way over ten minutes on your break. We're having a rush from that Lucas Theater musical review. All sorts of people waiting outside. Get moving."

Brianna stuffed her cell in her pocket and walked back to the bar in silence. She was really spooked now. What had happened over at Andi's home?

***

The inside of the Pirate's House was smaller than Morel had anticipated. Patrons were lined up waiting to be seated, many of them carrying programs from the Lucas Theater where the musical had just let out.

The trolley barker tried to get the entire ghost tour into the restaurant, but it was too crowded, everybody buzzing, some older gent quietly singing some fifties song, "one o'clock, two o'clock, three o'clock rock."

The only option was a short tour of the basement, a few dangerous moments on the steep, narrow staircase, no ghosts, and a few out-of-breath trolley riders, hastily back outside near the trolley.

"Sorry, folks. We're done here. Can't see the rest of the house or the restaurant, but let me tell you a story or two back in the trolley. This place has an awesome history."

The riders grumbled as Morel followed them back inside the trolley. The sirens had stopped now. Morel hadn't seen any police or fire vehicles, so whatever happened must not have been as big as he had thought.

He found his seat at the back, listened to the barker explain about sailors from the 1700s and some methods used to shanghai strong young men from the Pirate's House and take them out to sea illegally. Most of these methods used sheer force, drugs and violence.

The trolley was about a block from his home. Morel wondered if he could stop and get off now or would he have to take the whole tour?

***

Agent Stuart was yelling it, his voice hoarse as he and Gene ran to the back of the townhome, "Shoulda stopped him, shoulda stopped him."

They huffed around the corner then down the alley, the sound of the last gun shots in their brains. Sure, they coulda stopped him, but who knew? Joey was never violent to that extent, but, yes, he always took a gun. He made the females comply. They'd be close to hysteria. But, after the rape, they could be bought off, before they went to the hospital or the cops. Scared by his death threats. Taking his money. But this time something stupid happened.

Stuart spotted Joey first, the rapist ramming out the back door, slamming it shut, then running almost invisibly through the garden, the whole neighborhood sort of stopped in a suspended state. Of course, the neighbors heard the shots and some of them were probably dialing 9-1-1.

"Come on," Stuart shouted. "He's at the gate. We can grab him."

And sure enough, Joey was opening the garden gate in front of them, his clothes piled on one arm, his plastic bag in his other hand. And Gene took him down hard. "You little mother-fucker, what did you do? You fuckin' messed up." Rolling on the damp ground, Gene stifled Joey's protest, almost choking him with his own fury.

Dragging Joey back to his feet, Gene had his clothes. Stuart had his plastic bag. "Two guns? Two guns?" Stuart questioned the struggling mobster. "What the fuck! Why you got two guns in the bag?"

"Later, later," urged Gene. "C'mon. Let's get him to the car. Put some clothes on him."

Then, as they ran back down the alley, half-dragging the man, they passed beneath the street light. Gene could see the smears of blood on his own suit, and Joey's entire face and chest carried little streams of blood, fresh from the kill.

20

The Boyfriend

Morel got off on the corner of Oglethorpe and Habersham, but the intersection was blocked off to motorized traffic. He waved goodbye to the trolley barker and started walking west, confused by all the police and fire activity. *Must be a big fire or something.*

As he approached his own townhome, he was stopped by the jumble of ambulances and emergency vehicles. Police cars were scattered about the boulevard, even parking on the grassy median. The flashing blues, whites and reds gave the ordinarily calm setting a feeling of dread.

He approached an officer near the sidewalk. "What's up officer?"

The burly officer turned slowly, sized him up, gave a cop-like answer, "Can't say too much yet. You the one who called 9-1-1?"

"No, no, I was on the ghost trolley. Just got off. Where's the emergency… by the Conrad Aiken home?"

The officer, N. E. Singleton according to his badge, paused, started talking into the mic on his shoulder. "Yes, sir, Okay. I'll clear the way."

He set about moving his vehicle off the street and onto the median. Morel waited. A few more officers came to the immediate area, moving their cars off the street too. Then two ambulances began to zoom in Morel's direction, driving on the wrong side of the divided boulevard, their flashing lights turned on, but their sirens turned off.

After those vehicles passed by, Morel approached the same officer again. "Officer, was someone hurt?"

Officer Singleton looked directly at Morel. "Double homicide."

***

TJ was sleeping as a baby should, but Cat Gallaher remained awake, lying in bed, her eyes opened, then shut, then opened again. She was too excited to sleep, anticipating the arrival of Andi, Morel's ex-girl friend. Evidently, Morel had wanted to keep her in Savannah. But Andi wanted to get away from Morel and get on with her professional life as a physical therapist. She was dumping Morel!

Yes, Cat had offered to house Andi until she could get settled again. One of her generous moods, celebrating a small victory, but now she was having second thoughts. Why had she relented? She hated the whole idea of Andi, a talented young woman who took Morel from Cat and then tossed him away.

Yes, she was elated that Andi was out of Morel's life, but that didn't guarantee a single thing. Morel wasn't coming back to Cat. He was gonna remain in Savannah, hiding out, fearing to be caught, risking capture by the Feds each day. Soon, he'd probably get another woman to protect him, another freakin' younger woman.

Cat was nearing forty, a broken-down stripper. Morel was forty-four but still attracting women with his athleticism, his charming sense of hunor, his light-blue eyes. It wasn't fair. Couldn't he be loyal? Couldn't he get back to her and make things right?

She sat upright, the cool air-conditioned air brushing across her body, gooseflesh causing her to shiver. She popped out of bed, slipped on some shorts and a T-shirt, went downstairs to make some hot tea.

It was nearing 2 a.m. Andi would be just an hour away, speeding along highway 95, approaching highway 40, nearing Raleigh.

Cat looked for a snack, nothing but S'mores, graham crackers, Pop Tarts. All snacks for TJ, but they'd do. Soon, the tea pot was hissing steam. She put a Pop Tart in the toaster, pushed it down, grabbed the tea pot and poured the hot water over the herbal tea bag.

She popped up the snack before it was done, tasted the warm raspberry flavor, turned out the light and sat down with her snack at the breakfast table.

Outside, the bright neon lights of Deerrington Village pulsed against the sky. Living here had seemed like a good idea last year, before all the trouble. Now, the garish, youthful community seemed insulting to her, mocking her older self, forcing her to remember the good times with Morel when she had him in her arms, when every day was a good day, and when the sex with him seemingly went on all night. Now, each morning she was tired, restless, nothing going on but taking care of TJ and now she'd be taking care of Andi, the girl who had turned away from Morel.

She was nearing despair when her cell phone rang. *Must be Andi.* She pounced on the phone which was recharging on the counter nearby. "Hello."

"Cat. It's Palmer. There's been a tragedy down here. Andi's not coming back to Chapel Hill."

"Wadda ya mean? Did she get back together with you?"

Morel sobbed, "No, not that. It's… it's just that… Andi's dead."

***

Andi's mother and father heard about the shootings quickly. Agent Gene phoned them as soon as Joey had been hosed down, checked for injuries and then placed in protective custody at Hunter Army Airfield.

Agents Gene and Stuart searched some of the family's history on the net. Born in Pennsylvania, Andi had moved near Washington DC after high school with her two sisters, going to college at Georgetown where both her mother, Dr. Emily York, a well-known exercise researcher, and Dr. Clint York, a renowned faculty member in the School of Foreign Sevice, had taught for twelve years. While at the University, Andi had been a pre-Med major and a distance runner for the women's track team. It was in grad school at Chapel Hill that she became a physical therapy expert.

All of the Yorks lived in Alexandria, just south of the beltway, and kept a gorgeous pre-1820 home in the historic district.

What the Google resumes couldn't tell the two Feds about the Yorks' background was that Andi's parents were both also involved in clandestine activities, Clint working for the CIA and Emily as a researcher for the DEA, specializing in steroid abuse in professional sports.

When told of their daughter's death, the Yorks left immediately for Savannah, highway 95 not yet bumper to bumper.

Gene said he'd meet them at their hotel where all the Feds stay, The Inn at Ellis Square on West Bay. He had weaved a good story to tell them, all about Andi the good daughter gone bad. Not let them know too much. He couldn't wait to explain his cover story.

***

Clint York drove like a controlled maniac in his light-gray Chevy Impala, dry tears on his cheeks, his wife Emily crying herself to sleep on the back seat, her legs curled up as if she were a child.

It's different when it's your kid dead, lying in some morgue. It's different from assassinations, where the target is some mean son-of-a-bitch in Serbia. It's different when your best and brightest kid can't sing any of those old songs any more, those Carpenters' songs from the 1980s when Andi would pretend she was Karen Carpenter, beating on that little drum set in the basement, the one Clint got her because she had so much energy and enthusiasm. Thinking about Andi singing "Close to You" brought renewed tears to his eyes, and he struggled to keep from bawling out loud.

Goddam, someone is going to pay for this, he vowed. *Some bastard is going to be torn apart.*

Visions of Andi flooded his memory, the photos she had sent by email recently, with her friends partying in Chapel Hill, a photo of her running the New York Marathon two years ago, her first photo of her new boy friend, Palmer Morel, sprawled out in a hospital bed, his blond hair mussed, a funny photo (it must have been a joke) of her at the entrance of a tomb with the caption "My Bonaventure Cemetery Home."

The silence of the highway was punctuated by a stretch of bad road on the inside lane, the bump-bump of the tires on expansion joints irritating Clint until he pulled back into the fast lane.

But his brain continued with angry messages, clouding his emotions. *It's that Morel guy, he was a bad influence on Andi, taking her away from a job she loved, exposing her to danger, getting her to protect him. She told him she was leaving. She wanted out of a bad relationship. Morel probably has a bad temper. Maybe he had someone kill her? Maybe he's the one that planned her death?*

***

Morel stretched out in the crypt, only his dad's thin jacket under his head, his father's rental car parked on Bonaventure Street a good distance to the west.

It was just like his old dad to leave the keys in the car at the same time he was warning his son to be careful. Morel had retrieved the old jacket from the Buick's trunk along with a small arsenal of weaponry Pops was so proud of in a gym bag. His dad had left two guns in the bag, a 380 and a 9 mm. One gun seemed to be missing from the set, his favorite, a 25 mm baby.

But Morel's brain couldn't get around the significance of anything, his mind a jumble of images, yellow crime-scene tape, a battery of squad cars, ambulances, and then nearer to the shooting scene, mobs of cameras, TV stations, street people and neighbors.

Then the panic hit him again: one neighbor waving at him, a police officer looking his way, the feeling of doom, the horror of realizing the two bodies carted away were Andi and his dad, "dead at the scene" someone whispered close to his ear.

Dead. His Andi. His dad.

And then the fear had erupted. He had turned away, wondering what to do, spotting his dad's car parked on the other side of Oglethorpe, the hurt in his gut pounding, the urge for self-preservation taking over.

He remembered jumping away from the scne, then running across the broad median to the other side, in his eagerness to escape actually careening off the trunk of a large tree, falling down, scrambling back on his feet, getting to the car, opening the unlocked door and backing away from his home, trying to go slow, not attracting attention, his only thought was getting to Bonaventure, getting back to that crypt with the broken front door, the comforting stained-glass windows inside, hiding out again as he did last month. Hiding away from the danger.

After gaining some calm, he had called Cat at Deerington Village. Then, harder than anything, he called his mom back in Sedalia, woke her up, tried to remain calm as she asked him those questions: *are you all right? how's dad?*

And, then, remembering his answer. *Dad's not all right, Mom. I'm not all right. Someone shot Dad and Andi. They're dead now.*

21

The Big Lie

Cover-ups are always difficult, especially when the event is surprising, unusual, and involves a Federal contract with an unsavory, organized crime asshole. So, with no sleep and with wine hangovers fizzing their brains, Agents Stuart and Gene sat in the lounge of the Ellis Hotel on Bay Street, figuring out their plan, drinking Diet Cokes.

"Wadda ya think happened?" Gene asked.

"Just like Joey said," answered Stuart. "He was drugging the girl, a cell phone went off, the old man awoke, stood up and starting firing wildly. He somehow hit the girl with a bullet in the head. Joey ducked, then, he emptied his gun, killing the old man. Simple."

"Yeah, I know, but what about the cell phone call that spooked everybody, even Joey? I mean, who was it? Was it a signal to Morel? Was it our guys? Or should we be finding that phone, tracing the call?"

Stuart was always a little slow. "Oh, yeah. See what you mean. Could go public, viral on youtube somehow, person who made the call reports the crime. The locals get on the case. Hear of the different guns.

Hear of a scream. Gets out of our control. Shit, I don't know. Wadda ya think?"

Gene knew the first step. "Get the newspaper on the phone. Give our story-line. Don't mention two guns. Say it was an outsider broke in. Blame some guy. Some friend, maybe. A romantic friend. And we know who that guy is."

"Yeah, Palmer Morel, destined to be the patsy."

"Right. Get his name and description in the morning paper, on the local morning TV news shows. Get a photo of him, a wanted poster. That's the way we can control things, you know that. Set up the patsy first. Then we have time to give more details, set up the story real firm. Shit, we got both weapons."

"And then?"

"Well, then we get the phone at the home, trace the call, convince the fuckin' witness they heard it all wrong. Threaten the person if we have to, keep 'em quiet."

"What if they reported the call already?"

"Same thing. Saves us the time to trace the call. Get to the witness, bring 'em dowtown, quiz the hell out of 'em, scare them shitty. Take their phone as evidence. Lose the phone somehow."

"Yeah, but if they still wanna testify?"

"Well, they could have a tragic accident, maybe fall in the river on their way home. You know, lose control of their car. We can set that up easy. Get the mob to help. Joey's one of their's, isn't he?"

***

Brianna and Domingo were together again. The shock of the phone call to Andi busted up Brianna's usual rock-hard composure. Here she was, in Domingo's arms after the Plum Puddin' closed and neither of them could add much to assuage their fears.

"So, you prank-called her at the moment of a shooting. You heard shots fired?"

"Exactly, yes. I'm sorry, but that's what happened. I started whispering to Andi on the phone, some crazy shit about her babies would all die, so she screamed, and I heard loud pops, then nothing."

"Nothing. No shouts? No background noises, what…?"

"No, nothing cuz I got scared and hung up."

Domingo was incredulous. "So, you hung up, and then came to me, shaking like a fucking leaf."

"Yes, yes. That's it. Something happened bad, really bad, honest Domingo, I'm scared."

"Gunshots and then nothing. In my house? You know I rented that house to Morel and Andi. You know that? I'm in some deep shit now. A shooting in my house, and the Feds have been talking to Andi. The Feds fucking live here at night, and now I'm involved cuz I rented that fucking house to them?"

"I know, I know, I'm sorry, but that bitch kicked my fucking leg, she was a pain in the ass. I had to get even, scare her or something."

"Yes, yes. And fuck me, thank you. Do you know how much that house cost me? I was doing them a favor, and getting my house payment paid for. They said it would be a month or two, only, now I'm gonna be part of a shooting investigation? Jesus Christ."

"Nobody will know, honest. They couldn't know about me. Besides, I had nothing to do with it really. Did I? No. I called at the wrong time, that's all. The wrong time."

"Listen, if they find out someone called, they're gonna look at phone records. They're gonna get out their computers. They're gonna come over here and ask questions anyways. They'll talk to you. Do you know anything…do you have any knowledge of Andi, shit like that. They're gonna look in your eyes, see if you're lying. And, shit, if they ask me questions you better believe I'll say you were on the fucking phone with her. I'm not lyin' to the Feds. No way."

"Domingo, we gotta get a plan. Gotta do somethin'. We gotta stay out of this somehow."

"No, we're in it, we're in it good, and we oughta just go to the police. Say we heard about some shooting. Say we know the people, but that's it. Say we're sorry about whoever got shot, got injured, but we don't know nothin'. Then, we'll be fine, we'll be okay."

"Fuck, no. We can't do that. If the police look in my eyes, they'll see more than that. Like you said, they'll see guilt. No, no. I think I should get outta here. Go to Atlanta, some place like that. Shit, you know, disappear. But you can stay. You'll be fine. You just rented the house to them, that's all you did."

***

The Cuban landscapers were coming to work in their van. Heavy-set, swarthy Machio, paunchy, humorous Antonio, and the driver, grizzeled, gray-beard Miguel, stopped on Bonaventure Street to check out a new, red, rental car jacked up high, its four tires missing, the driver's side window bashed in.

"Enterprise Rental Car," said Miguel.

"Yeah, bad guys got to it good," replied Machio.

"That's crazy. Who would leave a car in this neighborhood over night?" asked Antonio.

Miguel pulled out his cell phone, looked at the Enterprise sign on the car's rear bumper, dialed that 800 phone number. "Yes, ma'am. I'm over on the east side of Savannah. I see an Enterprise rental car here. All the tires have gone missing…yes, ma'am, a new Buick, red,…license plate?... uh… Let's see… 522 RTR, North Carolina plate…on Bonaventure Street…near the Cemetery…what?...Bonaventure Cemetery…Look it up…okay…yes…you see it on the map?…okay…you're welcome."

"Did you ask about reward?" Machio was curious.

"No."

"Why not?"

"Don't want to…plus you guys are illegals. I don't want no trouble."

"We could get out, walk to work. You could wait. Get some money. Share with us. The American way, no?

But Miguel drove away, approaching their work station at Bonaventure Cemetery. Three years Miguel has been working here, and when his nephews came up last year from Cuba on a visa, he got them jobs with him…maintaining the beautiful cemetery. And Miguel was careful with their jobs, got them perfect ID's from a source in Atlanta, and now everything was fine. And they never went back to Cuba after their year was up.

"No problems with my decision, right, Machio?"

"Okay, okay, but I know you could use some extra money."

"Yeah, I guess, but who knows if I don't already get something extra?" Miguel gave his cynical smile.

***

James Barnard from the on-line newspaper, "Savannah Connects the News," wanted to write something about the killings on Oglethorpe, but the police were being very tight with the facts. No press conference until the afternoon, no comment on the reasons for the shootings, no victims' names, no nothing. In fact, Chief of Police Martin Gaston used the term "no comment" five times when Barnard talked to him on the scene.

Barnard himself had been walking home from the Lucas Theater where he was on assignment, covering the 50s musical review, when sirens led him to Oglethore just a few blocks away from his own home on West Perry. Without a photographer, he was somewhat limited for visuals, so he asked a number of citizens who were using their cell phones to email him their photos. He was busy at home now looking over more than 25 photos accumulating on his gomore@yahoo.com account.

On the desk in front of him was a photo emailed to him by the police department. It was a photo of a person of interest, Palmer Morel, a former tennis pro from Chapel Hill, North Carolina. Dressed in traditional tennis whites and armed with an older Jack Kramer tennis racquet, Morel looked athletic and handsome, a twinkle in his eye, a lopsided smile on his face. He looked like a nice guy, not a murder suspect.

Underneath the photo was the inscription, "Wanted for questioning in double homicide." And in the following text, the police urged the media to print the photo with a caption reading: "Armed and dangerous."

Something didn't seem right to Barnard. The police response resembled the same kind of approach used after a beating of a woman on Broughton Street earlier in the year. No mention of that police officer, but the woman's name and photo were released under the caption "Violent Drunk Slips and Falls." Afterwards, citizen videos revealed that the cop had actually knocked the lady down after Macing her first. Now, the cop was facing a trial and the complete police apparatus looks phony.

So, Barnard poured over the citizen emails, looking for police officers, possible suspects and for Palmer Morel in the crowd. Didn't mystery novelists insist that the perpetrator always returned to the scene of the crime?

22

Nice Legs

Daybreak. Muggy. No breeze in the crypt. Morel had left the door open a tad, but his sleep was full of spider nightmares, and he awoke startled, reaching for his legs, feeling for creatures.

Jesus Christ, what can I do now? He mopped the persperation from his face with his dad's jacket. He was dripping with sweat, his shirt stuck to his chest.

Got to pee.

He opened the door slowly, scanning the cemetery for the early workers whose mowers had often awakened him during the mornings he had spent here. He looked for food left in the crypt. Anything. But, now, all the amenities Andi had hidden for him before were gone, taken by somebody. The groundsmen took the stuff? No bottles of water. No snacks. No fruit. No towels. No bedroll. No beer. No extra money.

He went outside, hid on the dark side of the crypt and peed against the wall, finally relaxing a little.

Jesus. What am I gonna do? Dad. Andi. Dead. Who did this? Who? Wait a minute.

His mind changed gears. He remembered their special stash.

That's right. Over there against the crypt wall. That busted part opens up.

He reached inside the broken piece of marble and came out with a roll of fifties and hundreds. Couple thousand dollars. The Emergency money, Andi had called it. Just in case. In case he needed to get away fast.

I can take the back way through the grass along the river. Get back to dad's Buick. Get outta town. Go to New Orleans. Find a small place to stay. Get some money sent down from Sun Trust Bank. Would that work? Was that a good plan? Get away from here?

He closed the broken crypt door as tightly as he could, starting his walk down toward the river, hoping to circle back to Bonaventure Street, getting in the car and resting a bit, then maybe take Skidaway over to the Quick Trip, get some coffee.

There was no way he could stay at the cemetery any more. Too hot. No food. No one to help him. No one to keep him safe.

***

Journalist James Barnard needed to get some sleep. He'd worked all night. Now it was seven a.m. and his brain was slowing down. But he had one more option. Find out more about this Palmer Morel.

Google had told him something. Morel was an old-school professional tennis player, gave lessons in Chapel Hill. Had been involved in a shooting along the Haw River. Then dropped out of sight. Presumed dead.

Yet, here he was in Savannah supposedly, involved in another shooting, a police search looking for him, journalists being asked to write about him and a double homicide. Is Morel in covert ops for the military? Or are they setting him up?

Barhard decided to call one of his own street contacts, a guy close to the action with some mob and military connections. Should know more about Morel if there was more to know. A rich bartender at the Plum Puddin', Johnny Domingo.

He clicked Domingo's number on his cell, waited. No answer. He tried the Plum Puddin'. A recording. Too early for anyone to be there. He tried Domingo's number again. Domingo fucking picked up this time.

"What you want?"

"Johnny, it's me, your buddy, James."

"I know that. Says right here on my phone. Wadda you want?"

"You heard about the shooting?"

"Of course. It was at my rental property."

"You own that Oglethorpe condo?"

"James, wadda ya want? I got a big problem over here."

Barnard stopped to phrase his question just right. "Can I meet you for coffee?"

"Coffee? Now? Shit, I'm tired. Where you at?"

"At home. How 'bout Clary's."

"Is it open?"

"Hell, yeah. Six a.m. Can I pick you up?"

Domingo thought a second. "Okay, but I got a friend."

"A girl.?"

"Yeah, a waitress. She's bummed out."

"No problem. She can come along. You still living over in that condo on Price Street near downtown?"

"Yeah."

"Be there in five minutes."

***

Machio, dressed in high bright yellow/orange jacket, was running one of those silly, stand-up mowers down by the river when he first noticed the Morel guy who slept in the cemetery, the guy with the gorgeous dark-haired woman.

He slowed the mower, let the motor idle, tried to seem busy picking up some limb, tossing it onto the path. The guy saw him but kept walking away, toward the river, heading north.

Machio got out his cell phone, called Miguel. "It's your buddy," he said. "You know, the guy that's been living here in the cemetery, over by that Lawton graveyard. The guy with the beautiful, dark-haired girl, nice legs."

Miguel smiled, "Yeah, I know him. Never reported him did we. What's he doing?"

"Looks kinda lost. Don't have his girl-friend with him. He's still limping a little."

Miguel laughed, "Okay, okay. So what? Get back to work. He's harmless. Long as he causes me no problems he can stay here. I like his woman. We're doin' him and her a favor."

Machio wasn't satisfied, "I know, but…. maybe I should talk to him. Ask him if needs some help, you know, if he's got food, stuff like that."

Milguel was concerned. Machio was messing up with his secret operations. "Do whatever you want, but keep it short. It's supposed to rain later. I don't want that patch of lawn uncut for the weekend. Get back to work as soon as you can."

"Okay, okay." He started up the mower, revved it up and mowed a swath next to the path, following Morel toward the river, speeding up to overtake him.

Reaching Morel, he cut the engine again, letting it idle. "Sir. You okay? I mean, where's your girl? She okay? You and her need water, anything like that?"

Morel woke from his stupor, looking at Machio for the first time, trying to understand what was said over the *humm* of the mower. "What?"

Machio cut the engine off. "You okay? I mean, you still living over there in the Mitchell monument, you and your girl?"

A little scared, Morel opened the gym back to check on his dad's guns, and then approached the worker, one hand ready to grab a weapon. "You know about me living in here? You tell anyone?"

Machio shook his head. "No, we like you guys. Is okay you sleep here. You and your girl are welcome. Don't make no trouble for us. Is okay."

Morel took a deep breath, his sorrow close to the surface now. "I have to go. I might not come back here. But thanks for not telling anyone." He turned back to the path, heading out to his dad's car.

Machio yelled again as Morel moved quickly away, "Everything okay? Your girl okay?"

Morel stopped and turned, a helpless look on his face. "No, no. You don't understand. She's not okay. She died last night."

***

The Inn at Ellis Square was busy this morning, everyone looking for coffee, everyone in a hurry, it seemed, to get out and do some sightseeing.

The hotel provided the big Friday edition of USA Today and the local paper, The Savannah Morning News. Sipping their coffee, most were greeted by the brutal local story of a double homicide on

Oglethorpe. Then, next to the article, a picture of a "person of interest," tennis pro Palmer Morel.

The FBI had gotten their story out. Morel was depicted as a jealous lover, who was a person of interest in the murder of his girl friend and the accidental killing of his elderly father. The back story included an incident in North Carolina a few months before when Morel was shot near the Haw River, falling into the water and disappearing. Somehow, the story stated, "the wily Morel escaped death by hiding on the shore near Bynum, NC."

The Feds, Gene and Stuart, had happily read the slant of that story. Most of it they had dictated over the phone.

They were sitting in the alcove at a table with photos of Palmer Morel, Andi York and James Morel spread out in front of them.

On the other side of the table sat Andi's parents, the Yorks, trying to hide their angry tears. They looked at the photos, nodding their heads, but Gene could tell they were not thinking very well. Emily and Clint were grieving and Clint was also silently hysterical, though he struggled for control. He kept asking under his breath, "Where is he? Where is he? I'll kill the bastard."

Gene didn't know exactly where Morel was and, if he did know, he didn't dare tell York where Palmer Morel was, just yet. There might be a time when Clint York could be let go, but later, after some loose ends such as Joey Lingua were tied up.

"Well, Mr. York, we're searching for him. We know he was out on the town last night, having a good time, partying in Savannah. Some folks saw him on a ghost trolley, laughing and enjoying himself. We know when he returned to his home he was in a violent mood. Probably caused by alcohol. We know he fired that gun at your daughter and at his father when his dad went to protect Andi. But we must remember. This Morel is also an anti-American terrorist, shot and left for dead one afternoon a few months ago. Somehow, he survived, grabbed control of Andi and eventually took her life. We'll get him, make an example of him, but it takes patience."

***

Clary's was busy as usual on a Saturday morning, tourists waiting outside, and inside they were taking photos of the long counter where actors from "Midnight in the Garden of Good and Evil" had been seen on the big screen or lolling about as themselves more than ten years ago.

James Barnard escorted Domingo and his waitress friend, Brianna, along the outdoor seating and got an empty table far away from the door and the other tables. He let them settle down a bit, assuring them of his kindly intent.

"I just want to get the story straight before I print anything on-line. My deadline's at noon…so we got some time. My treat for breakfast."

The waitress interrupted them, they all ordered coffee. James got the eggs benedict, Domingo went with the classic eggs and ham and Brianna ordered the bagel with fruit.

Barnard placed his recorder close to them on the table. "Okay, ready? Tell me what you know."

Brianna lit up a cigarette and started first, her voice a bit too loud. "I can't tell you everything. But, Andi quit her job. She was going back to Chapel Hill. The Feds were in to talk to her. She got spooked. She was real annoying at work. I didn't like her, always late. I had to take her tables. She kicked me in the leg once. She was a real bitch."

Barnard stopped her. "Wait. Wait. You didn't like her. But you wouldn't want to kill her?"

Domingo interrupted. "Of course not. That's a stupid question. No reason to kill her. She treated the customers very well, always polite, a cute woman, lots of dash, you know, style, spirit. Lots of energy. Sass. Her boy friend came in once or twice. Nice guy. Big tipper. He took some shit from Andi, same as Brianna, but they seemed okay together."

"Jesus, right, no violence toward her," blurted Brianna. "Yet, you know, Morel might have seemed nice, but Andi was furious with him. I heard them talking. He was gonna take a new job. It was with Drayton trolleys. He was gonna be one of those talking guys, you know, a travel guide, tell the tourists ghost stories about Savannah, work at night. She hated that idea. I think that's why she was gonna move out. Morel might have shocked her. Then, maybe he reacted violently."

"Let me get this straight. For the record. You still seem a little angry yourself, Brianna. Did you know this murder was going to happen? Did you suspect something? Are those Feds you mentioned involved? FBI?" Barhard waited for her answer.

A big sigh. Brianna stubbed out her cigarette. "I'll tell you this much. The Feds were watching Morel. That I know. I don't know why. Morel was hiding out in Domingo's townhome on Oglethorpe. Andi wanted him to stay inside all day. Be safe. Morel disobeyed her. She got mad. That's it."

Domingo was ready to jump in. How much should he tell? But the waitress brought their food, Brianna started to munch on the fruit, and Barnard turned off his recording device. It was eight a.m. Barnard still had lots of time. And he still had a couple of photos to show them from the scene.

***

"Listen. Listen. Where you going? Can I help you?" Machio was very concerned. "Your pretty lady is dead? Listen. Maybe I help. Where you going?"

Morel put his head down, glanced up. "I don't really know. I've gotta get my dad's car over on the street. Then, damn, I just don't know. But, no problem. Don't worry. I'll figure it out." He started to walk away again through the tall grass.

"Wait. Wait, mister. You got a car around here some place?"

Morel paused again. *What the fuck?*

"Yes, I got a car. I gotta go now." Morel moved away but the mower followed.

"You gotta red car?"

More questions? "Yes, a red car."

The mower sped up, pulled along side of Morel.

"I think I know that car. You gotta big problem with that car."

Morel faced the mower. "I do? What do you mean?"

"It's got no tires. Tires all gone. Completely gone. Off. Someone steal them."

23

The Cabin

After his one call after midnight announcing Andi's murder, the redhead Cat Gallaher had no idea where Morel was, what he was doing. She didn't sleep at all. Finally at five a.m. she packed up little TJ from his deep sleep, wrapped him in a blanket and drove to the all-night greasy spoon, "Chill-Out," on Franklin Street in Chapel Hill.

The diner was shining brightly in the dawn, the greasy windows and neon sign bragging about "chicken, biscuits and okra." But all Cat needed was some coffee, and some hot cocoa and a couple of pancakes for TJ. The kid loved pancakes, could eat them every meal, and Chill-Out had his favorite syrup. He didn't mind the ever-present chance of getting hairs in his food (the cooks must never wear hair-nets).

Inside, the drunks had mostly cleared out and some students and early workers gathered comfortably at the greasy tables, chowing down the heavy fare. Near the door, the late-night cop stood passively near the door, took a big yawn, his eight hour shift almost done. Cat asked him if he had to break any heads tonight? He just growled and looked away.

She found a good table near a window, unwrapped TJ so his little head could peek out of the blanket, and he gave her one of his shy but pleased smiles. What a cutie.

She ordered and retrieved the food, then sipped her coffee, hot and black. TJ tore into the pancakes with his fingers, getting butter and syrup on his hands, cheeks and hair. OMG. She'd have to take him into the bloody restroom and clean him up before they left. She didn't want to enter that creepy-crawly restroom but there you go.

While TJ amused himself eating and drawing syrup pictures on his plate, she tried Andi's old cell phone again. Down in Savannah it was ringing, ringing, and then Morel was on the phone. "Cat. You okay?"

***

"So, are you ready to view the deceased?" Gene was blunt, but he had said everything he could think of, and The Yorks still hadn't calmed down. He'd need them later, maybe, during a trial, but if this was how they were gonna be, he didn't know if they could be trusted on the stand.

"Really. We should go. Get this over with. Put it in the past. Get some closure."

Well, that was a poor choice of words, and he knew immediately. "Put it in the past" was too blunt too soon.

Mrs. York burst into tears and Mr. York grabbed Gene by the throat, "Listen to me. Listen to me. That's my daughter. No fucklng Fed is going to call her an 'it.' An 'it'? Fuck you, Gene. That's my beautiful, talented, wonderful daughter and you're just some piece of shit!"

York let him go, giving one last push to Gene's chest, and the Fed held his temper, sitting down again, bringing out that perfected, toothy smile.

"Well, Clint, sorry. Didn't mean anything there about your fine daughter." A pause, then that big smile again. "You know, I lost a son in the line of duty. Over in Pooler, Georgia. A late night break-in at some grocery store. The perp still inside. My son went to the door. One shot. Right through his heart. I never really got over it. Bothers me right now. But, listen to me. We need to follow the procedure, look at the evidence, get your daughter's killer. If we stay calm, we can work through this. I know it will never ease the pain."

⁂

Prohibited from getting in to identify his father or Andi, and reading the morning paper which blamed him for their murders, Palmer knew now his dad's JFK warning was right. Palmer was the patsy.

He was stretched out on a lower bunk bed at a Tybee Island trailer park, his father's guns on the floor by his side.

The little cabin was quiet and primitive, room for four to six, unfinished wood, bunk beds, a master bed, a nice screened porch, far away from traffic. Just what he needed, temporarily.

It was Miguel who took time out in his busy mowing schedule to drive him to Tybee, leaving Machio to finish up at Bonaventure as a thunderstorm moved in. Miguel and the other workers made this place their home. The trailer park manager didn't bother them as long as they were quiet and kept the property clean.

Miguel promised Morel two weeks. That might give him enough time to get his head together, fix the funeral plans for Andi and his dad, and arrange for someone to meet his mom at the airport this evening.

After dropping him off, Miguel returned to Bonaventure, passed by James Morel's rental car and saw crime tape, police officers and "suits" gathered around the jacked-up car, dusting for prints, looking for evidence. It was obvious they were in a big hurry because the first big drops of the thunderstorm were splashing on the pavement and his windshield. They might lose the prints and other evidence if they didn't get on with it.

Miguel told Morel all these things on the phone, warning him to stay low out at Tybee. The police had also gathered in Bonaventure Cemetery, fanning out over the gravesites, looking for something or somebody, probably Morel.

Machio and the others had put the mowers away in the garage and were awaiting Miguel in the shelter while the distant loud boomers moved in from the southwest. Miguel said he'd try to get to Tybee within the hour, if they weren't detained by the police.

Sitting on the edge of the bunk now, Morel again looked at the newsaper and his large photo. The caption on his photo read "armed and dangerous." He had to agree that statement was the only truth in the entire news story.

***

A funny thing happened to Joey Lingua as he awoke at Hunter Army Airfield with his new military jump suit on, after his cold shower, after a short visit with an FBI handler who knew agents Gene and Stuart from the old days.

He sat on a lower bunk in Bldg. 100, some kinda barracks room, and found another blood stain on flesh side of his left hand near his wrist. He flashed back to the shooting and tried to remember where did this drop of blood might have come from. Must have been from Morel's girl. He never got too close to the dead old man, just pumped bullets in him from behind the girl's busted up head. This was her blood on his hand, near his wrist, a drop of blood resistent to the shower, the soap bubbles.

Using his right hand, he shoved his thumb nail under the droplet and popped it off like he might do with a beer bottle.

The dried droplet floated to the floor somewhere, not that he wanted it. He should find it though and flush it down the always open toilet. He didn't want to be tied to the murders. He didn't need to bother the FBI handler about it either.

It was good to have these FBI guys on his side. He told them how surprised he was when that cell phone rang and the girl screamed. Shit, he had shivers down his back, too. But he never expected the old man to start shooting. Damn, murder wasn't his style. He fired back in self-protection. He didn't kill the girl; the old man did.

Then he wondered: *why'd the old man fire at the girl? He never even looked at me. I was right there in front of him. I was drugging the girl. Why did the old man pick her for his target? I should be dead.*

His mind swerved away from that topic. Too scary. Instead he remembered his stomach. *Where's breakfast? Don't I get served around here at a decent hour? What's wrong with the military, man? Can't I get some service here?*

Almost like magic, he could smell some food, might be pancakes and bacon. That's what he wanted. But where was it and why wasn't he getting some now?

He could hear a loud thunderstorm approaching, but with no windows, the little room offered no opportunity to watch the storm arrive. He got up anyway and explored the room, opening up a chest of drawers next to the bed, nothing but a Bible inside.

He sniffed again and the smell of food tantalized him. When would he eat? He turned again to the chest and pulled out the Bible. Opening the book, he saw a stamped inscription, "Property of Andrea York."

What the fuck!

***

"Well, let's get it over then," said Clint York, his breathing settling down. If everybody knew his daughter was dead, why the fuck did he and his wife have to do the fuckin' ID? But he was fooling himself. He knew procedures. He had seen many deaths in his CIA days. But his daughter was something way different. Just hitting her stride in physical therapy. Just making some decent money. And then came this fuckin' Palmer Morel.

He sat in front with Gene. His wife sat behind him in the back of the big black sedan. "How far is it?" she asked.

Stuart also on the backseat answered. "Cross town. Going east. Then south past the historic district. Not too far. We'll take Waters Street south. Get to Memorial Hospital in ten minutes."

"And where's Andi being kept?"

"Right near the Emergency room. Standard procedure. Hold the body in an ante-room. Wait for identification. Find out where the body will be taken. You got a mortuary picked out after the autopsy?"

That did it. "Mortuary? We've been talking to you guys for an hour. You see me make a phone call? You hear me say anything about where my daughter's going to go? Jesus Christ."

After a silence, the big car rolled to a stop outside the emergency entrance. Stuart exited the car with the Yorks, went through the automatic doors inside to the waiting room while Gene parked.

Stuart introduced himself at the desk. Identified the Yorks. The gray-haired receptionist looked up. She spoke up loudly. "Shooting victim? Andrea York?"

"Yes, yes. Of course. Over on Oglethorpe."

"Okay, go down this hall right behind me, turn to your left, past the elevator. Dr. Stephenson's waiting for you."

"My partner's still outside."

"All right then. And….we received one message for the Yorks."

"A message?"

"Yes, sir. We had a phone call about the burial site."

"What do you mean?"

"We had a call about the burial site for Ms. Andrea York. The person informed us that Ms. York is to be buried at Bonaventure Cemetery along with the other shooting victim, Mr. James Morel. Both to be cremated. Is that correct?"

Stuart was a bit startled. "No, god dammit. What do you mean? No one's made any arrangements. We got the autopsy to be done. The parents are shook up. What are you talking about?"

"Well, sir. Morturary said the burial was all arranged. Paid for too. Oh, there's something else."

"What…else?"

"Another man's down the hall with Dr. Stephenson. Some kinda officer or something?"

"Police officer?"

"No, sir. Federal official of some kind, I think. Said he was a friend of the deceased young lady."

24

Biblical

Miguel was proving himself a real friend. Getting out to Tybee at noon, he brought Morel some lunch from Lighthouse pizza near the beach: a huge, thin-crust, mushroom pizza, salad, a local Moon River beer.

The wind was raking across the island, lightning flashing every few secnds, but Miguel raced onto the porch and inside the little cabin, a big smile on his face. "See, amigo. I didn't let you down."

After a minute or so of relishing each bite and sipping his beer, Morel had to smile. "Cannot repay you. Above the call of duty. Really, Miguel. Great stuff."

Rain pelted the windows and the cabin shook from a very loud crack of thunder. Then, briefly, the lights flickered, went off and came back on. "Close one," Miguel said.

"Very close. But we're good here. Did you eat?" Morel asked.

"Not yet. Too early for me. Later." He paused. "I saw something in Tybee."

"Something?"

"Somebody. A van. A big white van."

"Police?"

"Maybe."

"So, just sitting there?"

"Yep."

Morel felt trapped again. "I can't get away, can I? Even with your help, they're out there watching."

Miguel nodded. "They watched you at Bonaventure too."

"You mean yesterday?"

"Yes, but also ever since you moved into the crypt with your lady. Same van. Outside the fence or prowling around on the little roads. Same van. Every day."

Morel stood up, put the empty pizza box on the counter, walked around a bit, watched the rain come down outside. "They've been out there for a long time. Why the fuck don't they just arrest me, shoot me?"

"Back in Miami, Cubans say, 'haga el uso', to make use. They have reasons. Wanted to use you again. For something else."

"Make use? Set me up, you mean?"

"Maybe. Yes, maybe you take blame for these crimes. Wait till everything's ready. Then arrest you. Gather proof first. Paperwork. Witnesses. Or other plan, you resist, they shoot you."

***

Joanna Morel never wasted time. Growing up near Osawatomie, Kansas, she and her cousin Gretchen Sheldon shared an interest in guns and gardening. While Gretchen remained single, staying in Kansas, running the library in Paola, Joanna had found a man during her college career at Ohio State University, married him and moved to Ohio. She had always been an active Mom, just as her own history foretold.

All business, she usually lost control only for a moment. Her son, Palmer, had called to say her James was dead, so she cried for five minutes, and that was it. She immediately called KCI airport, buying a ticket to Savannah, then got in her husband's green GMC pick-up, and drove west the two hours from Sedalia to Kansas City.

The plane coming in from Dallas was late, but no worries. She parked the truck with the "Go Missouri" bumper sticker and ditched her one travel bag at the desk. The stocky older woman got herself a

Starbucks latte', chomped on a ham sandwich with pickles she had made in Sedalia, and pulled out her computer. Googling Savannah, she got the on-line newspaper and read about her son. She couldn't miss his big photo. And when she read his description and that horrid caption, she lost it again.

Jumping up, she screamed silently, her seventy-six-year-old lungs holding in a long screech into oblivion, the terminal nearly empty. She began to pace, working out a strategy. She'd get Palmer out of there. Get him back to Kansas City. She had some methods of her own. "Armed and dangerous" were not the words ever to be used to describe her son, but she herself could be a handful if pushed too far.

She placed two quick calls, leaving nearly identical messages. First, she called the editor of the Savannah newspaper: "You dumb shit. Leave my son Palmer alone." Then, she called the Savannah police: "You freakin' bastards. Leave Palmer alone."

When the plane arrived, she waited calmly, then marched back to her seat in 12A, putting her computer under the seat. She left a message on Palmer's phone before take-off. "This is your mom. I'll be in Savannah at 1:30. Pick me up."

***

Some army gal in tan army clothes came into his room. Joey suddenly got happy. "Yes, I want breakfast, and, hey, do me a favor. Just get hold of Gene Cooke or Stuart Moon."

"They're FBI, right?"

"Yes….they're federal agents."

"But you're not allowed. You're not supposed to contact anyone."

"Look. I don't give a fuck if I'm locked up…Wadda ya think? I'm gonna break out?....So, get me Gene. He'll know me. And bring me the phone here."

Luckily, Joey could get access to a phone, always, and he'd get it with his fuckin' breakfast. It would cost him some bucks, but the army waitress or warden or whoever she was seemed cool with it. Said she'd seen him before, said she worked a while over at the strip joint before she enlisted. Joey couldn't remember her face, asked her to raise her blouse, show her tits, help him remember her, but she refused.

Still before he could eat, he should get Gene Cooke here, show him the goddam Bible with Andi's name in it, for Christ's sake! But the food came, so he ate anyway, a good breakfast, eggs, bacon, pancakes, hot coffee. This mutha fuckin' army camp had its prioroties straight.

And after eating, Joey called Domingo at the Plum Puddin'. No answer, so he left a message. "Don't do nothin' stupid, Domingo. Don't say nothin'."

And then he had to call his wife, Molly. She knew he stayed out late and fooled around, but maybe she should know where he was. In case anyone asks, she'd have the facts and give the person the run-around.

"Molly, yes, it's me….goddamit, no…no…no, I ain't got no women…but listen, I am tied up for a while…no, nothin' like that….no fight…a misunderstanding…no, I ain't gonna be home today, I don't think…What? This guy wants to go to work now? You mean the guy, Morel? He phoned you today?.... The guy wants to start on the ghost tour? What the fuck's wrong with him….don't he read the papers?..What? Well, read the fuckin' paper…he's wanted for…..murder…. yes, murder…you want I should spell it out for you?...Listen, if the guy wants to work, set him up with George Arthur…yeah, the guy from England…let him work tonight, train with Arthur….Jesus, this is so strange…no, don't turn him in…it's okay…Hell, yes…I'll call you before I come home…bye."

Joey shook his head in disbelief, *Morel wants to work on the ghost tour? Unbelievable. Don't he have no feelings?*

***

The first message on his cell phone was short and Domingo knew it was coming. The detective was precise, "Mr. Domingo? You no doubt heard about the murders at your rental house? Call me immediately at the station, 888-555--1000. Detective Harris."

Domingo sighed. Brianna, still upset, was driving west through the thunderstorm to her home out in Garden City. The internet news reporter probably was writing up his story at his office. And Johnny Domingo took off his wet shoes and knew he needed some sleep. *But, what the fuck? Might as well get this call over with*, he thought.

He sat on a chair near the second-floor window so he could watch the rain. A real downpour. Tourists splashing in water up to their ankles in the gutters. He yanked at his wet, black socks, finally peeling them off. Punched in the police number slowly. Waited. A busy signal. He hit the redial. Still busy. What the fuck? He didn't have all day. Maybe he should just drive over to Oglethorpe?

But then the cop answered, "Detective Harris."

"Uh, yeah. I'm Johnny Domingo. You called me."

"Mr. Domingo. Good of you to call right away. We need you over here on Oglethorpe. Say, in ten minutes or so? You okay with that?"

"Should be fine. But I gotta be to work at 2 pm."

"No problem. It'll just take a few minutes."

"Okay, uh, do I need to call someone to, you know, fix the place up or anything. I read about the shooting. Blood? You know, any windows broken, anything like that? Call the insurance company?"

"No, no. It's secure for now. Investigators are still here. I can explain everything when you get over here. Park out back in the alley, okay? Come in the back door. We got Oglethorpe blocked off."

"Should I bring anything? Papers? The rental agreement? Anything to help?"

The detective paused, "Uh, yeah. Could you make sure to bring your cell phone along?"

Afterwards, Domingo listened to the recorded warning call from Joey Lingua. Of course, he'd be careful. What was Joey thinking? The mob could be worse than the fucking police.

Then he proceeded to erase every fucking message and contact off his phone.

25

Phone Tag

So, it was raining, Morel was in deep psychological trauma and was stuck on Tybee Island while his mother needed to be picked up at the airport. Miguel had gone back to get his workers at Bonaventure. There was no way Morel could get off Tybee on his own, except walk. He shoulda asked for Miguel's cell phone number. How could he get his mom at the airport? Call a cab?

Earlier, he had called the ghost tour owner, trying to tell the woman he couldn't work, but instead she ignored his excuses and assured him he could start tonight as a trainee. He asked, even if it's raining? and Molly said yes. Shit, the whole idea was crazy. His whole life had turned crazy. His photo in the paper and he'd be supposedly working the ghost tour tonight?

And earlier he made that hard phone call to Donovan's Mortuary. Hardest call in his life. Finding a place for his dad and Andi to lie for eternity. His mom hadn't said much, hadn't objected, but she wasn't happy with the arrangements. W*hy not Sedalia?,* she had asked.

Pops should have been buried in Sedalia. But it was so far away. Besides, he had already settled things at Bonaventure. Everything seemed too fast, unexpected, and the horror hung over him. Pops and Andi were here. Now they're gone. No goodbyes.

After paying with his credit card over the phone for the lot holding up to six graves, he arranged to bury Andi and Pops side by side, one for his dad, one for Andi. Settling the matter, he had relaxed a little. Mr. Richard Donovan had assured him, in greatest confidence, that no one would know who paid for the burial sites. But how could Morel know for sure? If the police contacted Donovan, wouldn't he capitulate? Of course he would.

But he still liked the idea of his dad and Andi being buried near the huge live oaks, the Spanish moss adding the feeling of finality and repose to the scene. Morel needed comforting, and that calm scene started to play over in his brain.

Then, he remembered Andi's Kia, still parked over near the Plum Puddin'.

***

Clint York could not say a thing. Of course, he recognized the man. Just the way he stood in the room, hands clasped behind his back, York noted his military bearing, his firm jaw, his perfect gray suit. The fucker was Sammy St. Julian, graduated Naval Academy 1972, Navy SEALs training at Little Creek, VA, action in Viet Nam 1973, then worked for the CIA 1974—Present.

Holding his temper, York strode across the room and shook St. Julian's hand after Gene Cooke introduced them. "Sir, pleased to meet you. We have word that you knew my daughter?"

St. Julian nodded, "Yes, I've known her off and on since her college days. Fine woman."

York stepped back a bit, looking down at the floor, his cheeks starting to burn red with anger. "So, you've known her eight years or so? How'd you meet her?"

"We both run, you see. I met her at a race in New Bern. She kept up a good pace, 10K run. Nice ponytail. Chatted with her for about a mile. Met her and her friends afterwards. I think we drank some orange juice, ate a bagel. Asked her if she needed a job. Gave her my card."

York grunted. "So, she called you, took a job?"

"No, no, but we kept in touch. I saw her race a few times in Georgetown. Good runner."

All of this was news to York, but he controlled himelf, called his wife over. "Emily, this is Sam St. Julian. He's known Andi a long time."

Emily took his hand, looked into his gray eyes, noticed the red tie, his dark tan, felt the strong grip, spotted the blue Navy Academy ring. "Mr. St. Julian, you got here before we did. Were you aware Andi was in Savannah?"

"Yes, yes. We've kept in touch. We were going to run the Rock 'n' Roll half-marathon in Savannah in November."

Emily shook her head, "No, no, I mean now, today, yesterday. You kept close to her?"

"We texted…frequently."

"So, did you know she was in danger? Did you know this man, this Palmer Morel she was living with?"

St. Julian nodded. "Yes, of course. We were watching him…watching his contacts. Your daughter was leaving him, you know? Going to move back to Chapel Hill before …before …her death."

Emily let out one loud sob, gained control. "So, you could have stopped … her murder?"

"I don't think so," St. Julian softly replied.

***

Agent Cooke watched this tortured conversation, until his cell phone vibrated. He hurried out the emergency door exit and answered. It was that damn Joey Lingua. "Wadda ya want, Joey? I'm busy."

"Damn right, you're busy. But I got another clue in the murder case. You can't keep me in here forever, you know. I'm fuckin' innocent, self-defense and you know it."

"What clue?"

"Listen, I'm lookin' through the chest of drawers here, the night stand, I dunno why, when I pick up this Bible, you know, an ordinary Bible in the drawer."

"Yeah, so what?"

"It's just a Bible but I look through it, I dunno why."

"You got a point here, Joey? I'm busy."

"Well, listen, have patience. So, I go to the front of the Bible and there's a name."

"A name, yeah. Whose name?"

"I don't have any idea why her name's in here, but it is."

"Whose name."

"Andrea York, the girl that got murdered."

"Andi York. Her name? Like she owns the book?"

"Yeah, yeah, exactly, like she owns the book or she was held here in this military prison one time, just like I am right now."

"I don't get it. What's the clue?"

"Just this. She ain't no ordinary girl."

"Her name in a Bible tells you this?"

"Sure. Sure. Do you see my point? This girl wasn't just no physical therapist with a hot bod, was she? She was important. She musta had some big-time contacts, you know, not just a Miss Little Innocent Victim."

***

So, yes, Morel had to call a cab, it showed up just down the road from the quaint little cabin on Tybee, and now he was ensconced in the back seat, telling the driver to take him to the Plum Puddin'.

He had Andi's key to the Kia on his key ring, he had his dad's mid-sized gun fron his dad's duffle bag in a backpack he "borrowed" from Miguel's room, and his emergency stash of money allowed him to be driven out south to book a room at The Oglethorpe Inn and Suites, off Eisenhower Road.

But as the cab entered the highway toward downtown Savannah, he spotted an old white van in the rear view mirror, just behind the cab a few car lengths, trying to keep pace. So, even now the "watchers" were keping up with his moves, yet seemed unwilling to pick him up, arrest him or shoot him. Odd.

"Driver, we're being followed by that white van. Did you notice it when you got to my cabin?"

The driver, a sloppy-haired guy with a very-dirty, thin neck and a backwards orange Clemson cap, said, "No, sir. Dint see nobody. You think he's following my cab? Any reason?"

"Well, it's been around my house. I've seen it a couple days now. Never could see what the guy looks like, though. Maybe I'm just paranoid."

"Can't be too careful, sir. Break-ins. Robberies. Quite common on the east side. You do any business off the island, maybe down around Skidaway or Bonaventure street?"

"A little. You say some guys follow people to, what, rob them or find out where they're going?"

"Yes, but I've also heard of PI's spying on men involved in divorce cases. Is that your situation?"

" Not exactly…but I wouldn't want him following me once I get out of the cab. Is there some place you could drop me off so I could get out and leave unseen? Some building I could cut through? Some other way to get away from that van?"

The driver coughed. Took off his hat, smoothed his sticky blond hair, put the cap back on. "I can't speed away from him, can't break no laws if that's what you mean. Say I don't drop you off near the Plum Puddin', huh? Then, how 'bout I drop you off in the market, then you can mingle with the tourists and get back to the Puddin' on your own?"

***

The yellow crime scene tape was still around the condo, and Domingo followed police instructions and drove up the alley instead, parking just outside the familiar backyard.

He expected masses of police everywhere searching for clues, but the neighborhood was very quiet, just one black police car out back, no officers visible anywhere.

He closed and locked the car door, then remembered his cell phone on the passenger seat. He re-opened the door, reached over and put the phone in his pocket. He knew why the police wanted it, but why argue. He had already erased any messages or addresses he had saved. What could they find now?

He opened the gate, crossed the yard and got in through the back door. He walked down the hall to the living room, but that room was blocked by crime scene tape, so he called out, "Harris, Harris. I'm here. Where are you?" He had expected to chat in the living room, but now that was impossible, so he waited, tapping his right foot to some internal nervous beat.

Finally, an answer. "Mr. Johnny Domingo. That you? I'm upstairs. Come on up." Domingo heard the toilet flush.

Domingo took the steps two at a time and wound up almost running into Harris at the top of the stairs when Harris stepped out of the bathroom. "Whoa, you okay, detective?"

Harris was not the red-faced good ol' boy he expected. No, Harris was young, with that cool look of a Duke University starting basketball guard, short black hair, perfect white teeth, a kinda sarcastic smile always on his face.

"Billy Harris," he said shaking hands. "Good of you to come, Johnny. Did you bring that phone?"

Domingo reached into his pocket, started to give the phone to Harris who hesitated. "Wait a second." Harris pulled out some gloves, put 'em on, then took the phone. "Sorry, got to check for prints in case someone else has been using your phone." He slipped the phone into an evidence bag. Closed it up, then gave Domingo another sarcastic smile.

"Listen, detective. I have nothing to hide. I'm just as shocked as you about these deaths. Andi was a good worker, a fine human being. I rented them the condo as a temporary favor, until they could get settled some place else. I have no idea who coulda killed them."

Harris nodded, "I understand. But could you take a few minutes, look around here and then downstairs. See if anything's missing or disturbed? Anything that doesn't look right?"

"I gotta be to work in about an hour."

"No problem. You're free to leave when you have to. Just be as thorough as you can, okay?" Harris took out a note pad. "Just tell me anything you see."

26

Self-Fulfilling

The first look was bound to be traumatic, and it was, Audi on the table, covered only by a sheet, her beautiful head now misshaped eerily, her black hair cleaned up a bit, but with clotted areas where most of the blood was gone, but the hair was still spiking up unnaturally.

Her father observed quickly, the single shot through her head, an instant kill. He said nothing, holding his anger, but his lips quivered into an ugly grimace, a moment of resolve.

"I'm ready," he said loudly, but ready for what was only implied. He turned abruptly away from his daughter's body and strode resolutely out the door. Agent Greene followed.

York continued to speak forcefully when outside the door. "If you can't do it, I will," he warned, his eyes vacantly focussed on the gray wall.

Greene nodded, but replied, "Not really, sir, Not really. We know the man responsible. He'll be taken into custody and he'll go to trial."

"No, he won't," York said.

***

Morel had only a fistful of fifties and hundreds. He peeled off a fifty, gave it to the cab driver and stepped out near Johnny Mercer's tiny statue in the market plaza. Tourists walked by eating ice cream cones, some music played down the block and horses tied to tourist vehicles snorted, their bodies sweating from the early afternoon's heat.

He had forty-five minutes to get to the Kia and drive to the airport. His mom would be gazing out the plane's window now from her seat, impatient to land at Savannah International Airport, upset yet determined. Losing her husband would be a nightmare pushed deep into the back of her brain. Her primary goal would be to rescue her son, get him safey back to Sedalia. But Morel would need to squelch her idea quickly. Nowhere was safe for him, and some sinister forces still lingered nearby, waiting to play another dirty trick on him. Going to small-town Sedalia would not work. No hiding places.

Checking Reynolds Square for watchers, Morel walked past the Kia once, passing the Plum Puddin'. He circled around the square quickly, got the driver's side door open, started the engine and crawled slowly toward Bay Street.

He swung off on highway 25, hit 21 out by Garden City and then entered the airport off Gulfstream Road. His mom would be getting her luggage. He parked the Kia outside the luggage area, hopped out of the car and down to the luggage area.

There was his mom waiting for the circle of baggage trunks to go around. She was dressed in those ancient, baggy yellow shorts he remembered from years ago and that light blue Tar Heel T-shirt he had sent her for Christmas. Together with those scruffy white, grass-stained tennis shoes and a yellow visor she used for gardening, she could pass for some exotic plant.

He called out, "Mom," and she turned slowly, reaching one hand out for her passing bag, the other up in the air waving at him. She was quite a trip.

***

"Don't give me that," she was saying, still chewing on some french fries after a quick trip to Mickey D's. "Your dad was more than an old fogey. He had you fooled was what it was."

Palmer was heading back to Savannah, driving slowly for his tastes. His mom insisted he use the far-right slow lane, and he was getting caught between semi-trucks and slow cars trying to merge.

"No, no, I don't mean fogey or geezer. I just mean it seemed he had slown down a little. His quick wit, his memory, just slowed down."

"Nonsense. He was still sharp. Now listen. I'm gonna tell you a few things about your dad you never knew. I don't know all of it either, but just listen to me."

"Geez, mom. I think I know all about dad."

"You don't. Not even close. I don't care if you had a heart-to-heart talk with him down here. I gotta tell you some things now. First, your dad was in Viet Nam, the shooting war, right before you were born."

"Knew that mom."

"Don't be a smart ass. You know nothin'. Dad didn't stop with the military after the war. Didn't stop at all. He'd get a strange call, middle of the night, and he'd have to leave."

"What kinda call?"

"Wouldn't even tell me much. Would just say, 'Special ops.' That was it. Be gone a few days. Come back all disturbed. Would sleep by hisself then. Kinda shook when I'd hand him his coffee in the morning."

Palmer thought about that one. "Okay, got me on that one, that's new. But he ever tell you what was goin' on?'

"Never. Never. But I figured it out."

"You did?"

"Yeah, kind of put it together myself. Reading the paper, watching the news. No photos of dad or anything, but I started clipping news events after dad would leave."

"So? What was goin' on?"

"It was all them assassinations in the 1960s and 70s. Right after dad would leave, there'd be one of them assassinations in the paper."

"What? Dad was involved?"

"In some way, yes. King, the Kennedys, Evers, Reuther, Wallace, the Kent State shootings. All occurred right after dad left on some trip."

"What? That's crazy. You think dad shot these men?"

Mrs. Morel scoffed, "Hell, no. Your dad was no sharp shooter. He was a driver over there in Viet Nam. He drove vehicles, trucks, motorcycles, cars. He was an expert. That's what he did at those murders. He was a driver for the shooters, for the patsys, for the second, third, or fourth dummy car used to put the police off the track. That's what he did. He aided and abetted."

Palmer was stunned. "Mom, I can't believe that. Dad was a kind-hearted guy, not a killer. Shit, he wouldn't step on a spider. He wouldn't give me a spanking. Impossible."

Mrs. Joanna Morel rifled through her purse. Brought out a 8 by 10 computer copy. "Found this on the internet just a couple years ago. Only photo of your dad I ever found in the press or on-line. Look here at this crowd scene. What do you see?"

"Hey, I can't look now, mom. I'm driving, did you forget. There's too much traffic on the highway. Let me look at it when we get lunch in a couple minutes, okay? We'll grab a sandwich over where I had a beer with dad the last time, the Moon River Brewery."

"Look at it," she screamed.

He took a peek. There was his dad on the street in Dealey Plaza as JFK's limo passed by.

***

Clint York let his wife take a nap at the hotel. But for himself, he needed a walk, a long walk on Bay Street. He put on some tan shorts and a blue T-shirt, a Senators ball cap. Took the elevator to ground level. Walked out into a bright blue sky.

The memories kept coming: Andrea doing finger-painting in kindergarten, an orange-red fire scene at a pretend cartoon mall; Andrea running through the backyard chasing her pet dog "Snoozy"; Andrea picking a violet and plunking it on his desk in front of him as he typed; Andrea finshing her first 5K race in 21 minutes; Andrea giving him a big hug after she got her doctorate in physical therapy.

The tears came, of course, and York took off his glasses, got his handkerchief and wiped his eyes, tourists walking by him on the rough brick road near the river, the smell of good food in the air, a large tugboat chugging up the river.

The sun was blinding him now, the sun lowering, its reflection on the river giving York a double-dose of brightness. He hustled as best he could down an alley between the former warehouses and found some steep steps back up toward Bay Street.

He could use a beer.

Across the street was a pub, a brewery-restaurant called Moon River which also announced on its façade the chance to drink some local brew.

The last time York visited Savannah he had been on a job, checking with local police and the mob about certain sailors from Poland from a large container ship who had skipped out and had been hiding somewhere in the river distrct.

The Moon River Brewery had not been built at that time; in fact, all of Savannah had been pretty shabby, old, gorgeous homes being torn down to make way for....parking lots.

York remembered a song from that time and its words flashed across his mind: "Pave paradise, put up a parking lot." He had thought that song to be very left-wing, hippie-dippy stuff when he first heard it. Now he agreed with its sentiments. Greed had entered the American business community at a level unheard of years ago.

He watched the crossing signal count down as he walked across Bay Street and headed toward the Moon River. Entering, he had some difficulty seeing in the dark atmosphere, but then headed toward the brightness of a window seat. He could drink a beer and watch the tourists pass by.

***

Brad Hollofield had called Cat Gallaher from Charleston and both agreed. The double-murder in Savannah had made the national news. So had Palmer Morel's photo-bio. It read like the bio of a serial murderer: a loner, a selfish tennis player, a womanizer, a trail of dead bodies. Even some quotes from former tennis players and tennis students, all alluding to Morel's lack of roots, his travel across the

United States for no obvious reasons, his possible ties to organized crime.

But one quotation used in USA TODAY from the Deerington Tennis Club in Chapel Hill got Cat's Irish blood boiling. One of Morel's middle-aged tennis students, the notorious Dolly Minori, stated: "Morel and his red-headed girl friend, Cat Gallaher, are nothing but sex sluts. Pretending to be helpful, they take, take, take and ruin everything they touch. He faked his own death in the Haw River and then the two of them seduced that little physical therapist, Andrea York, and got her involved in their dirty sexual games."

The accompanying photograph from last summer showed Cat, Brad and Palmer huddled together at the swimming pool after a softball game, Cat's breasts almost falling out of her bikini top.

"Cat, we gotta get over to Savannah. Help Palmer get outta there."

"I agree. And I'll try, but I've been watched every time I do anything."

Cat said, "Listen. They'll follow you but so what? Just do it." Then, she worried a moment. "But wait. You've got warrants. They'll follow me and get you."

Brad agreed, "Yeah, but I don't have a life here anyway. Maybe all of us can work together. Prove our innocence."

Cat laughed. "Well, okay, if you're game. I'm really angry and ready for anything. I'm fucking leaving right now. I'll pick you up. Where should we meet?"

"Just off highway 26. I'll wait at the off ramp at Remount Road. When will you get here?"

"I should be there by seven pm. Oh, shit. What am I gonna do with TJ?"

She gave Sara a call.

27

Mixed Ops

"Of course, they're stupid. Ridiculous. Do they think we don't know where they are, what they do?" asked Colonel Max Melty as he stirred his beef stew. He was sitting in the low-brow restaurant, Perkins, on 64 highway near the town of Apex. He didn't care about fine dining. He stopped into Perkins any time he was in the neighborhood. He liked the idea of the pot of coffee on the table, the happy waitresses, the senior citizen discount. There was always a Wake County Highway Patrol car in the parking lot. A good place to share ideas, settle some things.

"No, I agree. The Patrol doesn't have jurisdiction, but we can take part in the arrests….What?....I know. I know. Murder One is off the table, but Hollofield was an accessory. We can nail him on that…..You mean that Gallaher lady and the little boy?.....Okay, yeah, I can see that, but what will we do with the kid?....Wait a minute. Is there money for that in the budget? The Tea Party's cut back on social services in North Carolina, you know….Well, I feel sorry for the young kid. No parents. ……Okay, okay. We go down there, help out, take custody of the kid, bring him back here….I'll get down there now. Get my driver,

Ken Niquist….Yeah a probationer…Of course, he's dependable, but kinda liberal….When?….No, not yet…Hey, just lemmie finish my stew. We got some time, don't we?....Course I know it takes five hours to get to Charleston ….It's 2 pm ….We'll be there by eight."

***

Back to back in separate wooden chairs, by the window, both looking outside, drinking a beer, that's how Joanna Morel saw the two of them. One her son, grown into a nice looking man, had her long blond hair, her blue eyes. The older man looking away she spied on was obviously some sort of Federal officer nursing his beer, his gray hair neatly cut, his body getting older but his physique still in top shape for his age.

    She felt strange, odd, and she couldn't talk now that the big older guy had sat down behind her son. She knew this guy was a Fed, but couldn't place him. Some contact from the past, when he was younger, when he knew her husband, James. Near as she could figure, he probably was in town because of James. Was he the one who called on the phone that night in Sedalia, just before her husband took the trip to Chapel Hill, then to Savannah? Is this the guy who set her husband up with some job to do here?

    She reached her left hand over to touch Palmer.

"What's up, mom? Need another beer?"

She shook her head, put a finger to her mouth, then mouthed, "Let's go."

"Now? Our food hasn't arrived. What are you talking about? You were gonna show me some photo."

Rolling her eyes, she shook her head. After a moment, she got up, pointed toward the rest room and left the table.

Morel nodded now, thinking she just needed the restroom, and he took another deep gulp of dark beer, watched the folks walk by outside.

But then he noticed his mom return to the bar, wrapping up their hamburgers and fries in "to go" boxes. She waved at him when she was done, and then she scooted out the door.

Morel took a last hurried sip of good beer, put the glass down, and followed her outside.

"What the hell, mom? We just got there."

His mom took off going east on Bay Street, not stopping to talk.

"Mom, will you tell me what's goin' on, please?"

***

Building 100 was no fun. Joey's buddies, his FBI agents, were letting him sit there in the room, no messages, nothing.

What about the Bible? Wasn't that something new in the case? Didn't that prove something about Morel's girl? Of course it did. Yes. She was here. She had military ties, FBI ties. She was a player. She was a Fed.

Pacing didn't calm him. Joey tried calling his wife again, but no answer. Did she have her phone turned off? Not likely. Was she taking care of business. Not likely. And that Morel wanted to work tonight, wanted to do the ghost tour. Remarkable. He's involved in this whole plot, the plot to get Joey and keep him locked up.

"Officer, officer," he started shouting. "Let me out of here. I got work to do."

***

"We'll go to our Inn, Palmer. Just get us out of here. Get us to the motel and I'll explain. Just get moving. This is much more dangerous than I ever knew. It's just inconceivable, horribly inconceivable."

Mrs. Morel held the to-go boxes on her lap as her son turned the Kia through the Savannah squares, this way, that way, a stop, a go, a trolley blocking the way, so many cars leaving now for their homes south of town, a horse and carriage, a young couple smiling, Abercorn Street full of cars and students and tourists, and Mrs. Morel's head shifting with each turn, her hands holding tight on the boxes, her mind working to figure things out.

It was impossible to drive fast. Palmer tried it, but there was no way. Traffic was backed up. Everyone in a hurry to get home. At the stoplight on Stephenson, he looked at his mom next to him, her head straight ahead, her face frozen in a grimace. *She's not talking. She's not talking. She always talks. What did she see? What has happened?*

"We're almost there, mom. A few blocks. Are you okay? What's wrong?"

"I'll tell you son. I'll tell you. Get us to the motel. Go. The light changed. Go."

***

It was Samuel St. Julian calling on his cell. Clint York knew the fucker would call. "Yes, Sammy. Go ahead."

"I had to call you."

"I know."

"I had to call before you did something rash."

Sitting in the Ellis Inn lobby on Bay Street, York sighed, "I'm not ready to do it now, but, yes, I'm thinking about it soon."

St. Julian talked softly, "Don't do it. He's not the one."

"You mean Palmer Morel?"

"Yes, he's not the one. There was a different operation going on."

York paused, then, "You mean on my daughter, your protégé? You fucker, did you do it?"

St. Julian calmed him. "No. No. Not me. I was just as shocked, just as broken down about it, believe me."

"Goddam it. Not Morel? Then who?"

***

After a short nap, Palmer's mother was still upset, but ready to talk. She had joined her son in his room, and both sat on the couch in the divided little suite. Morel had some hot coffee for them, and as they sipped, his mom told the story of his dad's secret life.

First, she again pulled out the photo her son had glanced at in the car. It was a famous photo, one Palmer had seen before.

"I saw that mom. I know and that's Dealey Plaza, Dallas. It's an old photo of the assassination."

Mrs. Morel said, "Of course. We've all seen it, but look here." She pointed to the parade route, the spectators watching as Kennedy's car turned on its fatal journey.

"See, everyone's happy but one man. Can you see? The man's not smiling. He's just standing by the road, not happy at all."

"Yes, mom, I saw it in the car. I see it now. So?"

Mrs. Morel smiled slightly, "He's younger there. That's 50 years ago. Palmer, that's James your dad. He was in Dallas on military assignment, just before the Viet Nam War got bigger."

Palmer looked closer, "I don't think so, mom. Doesn't look like him. How do you know for sure?'

"We were just married. He had to report for active duty in a couple weeks. He had done special training at Fort Bragg and he was home for a week. Then, he got that phone call in the night. We lived in Columbus, Ohio. He said Fort Bragg called him. He left immediately. The next day I heard about the assassination. Your dad returned a couple days later, the same day Jack Ruby killed Oswald."

Palmer was confused, "Dad shot Kennedy?"

"No, no. I told you he was a driver, one of the drivers. He parked his car behind the fence in the parking lot by the grassy knoll. After the shooting, he drove one of the shooters away, to safety. The guy was never caught. Your dad was never interviewed by the Warren

Commission. They never got the facts, never wanted the facts. It was our right-wing military had JFK killed."

Palmer asked, "But why'd we leave Moon River so fast?"

Joanna waited, then, "One of the men. The special ops. The assassinations. A man sitting behind you at the restaurant was involved in all of it."

28

Power and the Press

The on-line newspaper "Savannah Connects the News" had a reputation for digging up the facts quickly, so when the James Barnard story of the killings was put on-line, the Savannah PD noticed immediately, especially Detective Billy Harris, lead investigator on the case.

The murder house on Oglethorpe had not yet been cleared by the investigative team when supposedly secret stuff was being revealed to Savannah at large.

Harris noticed the on-line newspaper had posted Palmer Morel's wanted photo earlier in the day, getting hundreds of responses and sightings, just as the police had hoped. Now it had been taken down and a new photo was posted. Under the headline "Public Owed Explanation", an old, black and white mugshot of Joey Lingua graced the front page. The story was no less sensational.

Along with Joey's mugshot were five photos taken near Oglethorpe Avenue immediately after the double murder. The e-mailed photos were lined up sequentially even though taken from different angles by different witnesses. These photos had not been seen by the local police. Only the Feds could have released them

The first photo showed two, large white males wearing suits half-carrying a semi-nude man from an alley. The second and third photos showed the half-naked man still being carried south toward Oglethorpe. The last two photos, one a close-up, showed the same men walking south through Colonial Cemetery. The close-up seemed to reveal the identity of the naked man: Joey Lingua.

The story itself used confidential sources to reveal two startling facts supposedly known only to the police. One of the murder victims had received a threatening call shortly before the shooting. Second, the murder house was owned by a well-known mobster, Johnny Domingo.

Detective Billy Harris was not pleased. *Who the fuck has leaked this information?*

***

Palmer's mom had the room next door on the second floor, 203, at the Oglethorpe Inn and she was sleeping again. He had 205 and was looking out the window to a nearly empty parking lot at the back. He really shouldn't leave her alone, but he was restless. The information she gave him about his father was really, really too much to absorb.

Using Andi's old phone, he tried to get hold of Cat, but she was unavailable. He left a message, "Call me," and that was it.

In a moment, he tried Cat again and she answered. "Hello, Palmer. You okay. We're worried."

"I'm fine but confused. You been reading the news."

"Damn right. Brad and I are on our way from Charleston. Almost there. Where are you?"

Palmer shook his head, "You what? On your way? God, Cat, is that a good idea?"

"We both decided. If Andi and your dad are dead, only we know it's not you that killed them. All the newspapers have your photo as the killer, even USA TODAY. We stick together, Palmer. We'll help clear you."

"My mom's here."

"She flew in from Sedalia?"

"Yes, and she's a brick."

"Really? How does she do it?"

Morel hesitated, then said, "She knows a lot about what happened here. My dad was involved. I'll tell you more. You know Savannah better than I do. Any good place we can meet when you get here?"

"Of course, silly. That's why we're came down. Let's meet at, where? Brad says the Pirate's House. In a half-hour. You know where that is?"

"Yes, but….I got a better idea. You won't believe this but I start a new job tonight at six. I'm supposed to work on the ghost trolley tonight. Can you guys meet me at the Trolley Stop at the Welcome Center? There's parking there."

***

There was a quiet conversation going on in the coffee house on Habersham Street. Both federal officers and the local Savannah police were involved.

"Billy, you're in over your head. We are involved in the cover story. We released those stories and photos about Joey," said Agent Gene Cooke. "I was one of the men carrying Joey from the scene. Stuart Moon here was the other. We got a long list of Lingua's activities. He's a terrorist. We're gonna hold him."

Detective Harris sipped his coffee at a table at Clary's, trying to hold his temper with these two men. "Terrorist? We got him listed as being mobbed up. Sure, he's a rapist. We got his records. He's never been outta the country. All his friends are involved in topless places, pornography, gambling. Terrorist? You gotta be kidding."

"Listen, Billy," said Stuart, reaching across to touch Billy's arm gently. "We're on this case now. We got Joey over at Hunter AFB. We're picking up Johnny Domingo at his restaurant tonight. We got the goods on him, too. They'll be kept out at Hunter until we can move them over to Leavenworth, Kansas."

Harris put his coffee down. "You got them on terrorist acts? What charges exactly? Those murders at Domingo's townhouse? Blowing up buildings? What?"

Gene shook his head, "No charges yet. Patriot Act says we can keep 'em locked up without charges while we investigate. For your own purposes, you can say they're connected with Al Qaeda or foreign operatives if you want."

"That's impossible."

Agent Stuart Moon spoke simply, "We talked to your boss, Billy. Chief Detective Al Ammens, down at the station? Says you're a good kid, but a bit impulsive. Says you're lookin' for a promotion soon, right? Married? Two kids? That right? Anyways, we cleared this stuff with him. Now, he said you need to relax. Take it easy. Says we can have that evidence you collected, those guns, those blood samples, and anything else you got."

***

James Barnard had it all now. Praise from his editor for his persistence. Congratulations from the Savannah Chief of Police for unearthing a terror plot. A text message from Hunter AFB commending him for bravery, "gud job!"

The only downside was an earlier 3 pm phone message from Johnny Domingo yelling at him for getting him involved with Joey's problems. But, shit, Domingo had nothing over him now. He'd be arrested soon by the Feds. He'd be sitting in a cell at Hunter AFB himself.

James Barnard felt guilty as hell. Something wasn't right. Mistakes and lies had been made. And, yes, he had been the one to get dirtied. He had been told to ignore evidence, change evidence, falsify the story. And he had followed orders. But he had to. Patriotism demanded it. He'd do anything for his country.

Trying to assuage his conscience, he picked up his cell phone, called waitress Brianna Taylor. "Hi, Brianna?.... Yeah, it's James Barnard......Yes, I wrote it...I'm sorry....Well, yes, the photos were real. Those were actual federal agents with Jocy...No, no, no....Nothing about Johnny......No, nothing about you...I left all those names out...No, I don't know why they did that...Right, right, it's not the Savannah police, it's the Feds...I'm really, really sorry...I know those guys aren't terrorists, but what can I do? .....Listen, once the Feds get 'em they'll get no attorney, no rights....Sure, I'll testify if I'm called, but....No, I didn't know you and Johnny were like that...You never told me...No, he never told me. How could I know you might get married to him?...Call him if you want, sure.....No, it won't help....What?....No, they'll just track him down."

Barnard now felt like shit. *First, I got all that praise for an unethical story. Now Brianna and Johnny are caught up in it. Jesus, how fast things change*, he thought. *How can I get myself out of this?*

***

Trooper Ken Niquist couldn't drive fast enough for his boss Max Melty, but if he went any faster he'd be ten miles over the speed limit and he wouldn't get pulled over in South Carolina for anyone. "Sir, I know we're in an unmarked car, so these SC troopers will pull us over for sure, and we'll be on the nightly news. You want that?"

"Listen, Trooper. I know you're on probation with the Patrol, but don't worry. I'll back you up we get pulled over. Each Highway Patrol protects its own no matter where we are. Now go at least eighty so we can get to Charleston tonight, not next year. Now move."

So, Niquist hit the gas, got the Dodge Charger old black and silver up to eighty and zoomed past the "South of the Border" billboards along I-95 like a dream-sequence out of the movie animation from "Cars."

"I don't know, Colonel. This speeding is making me nervous."

The Colonel broke open another sack of Doritos, said, "Just drive."

***

Johnny Domingo was munching on a pulled pork slider with some slaw, trying to get his head around his situation. He just got done talking to Brianna and she was all upset.

The night crew was just arriving, full of life and gossip. He stood behind the bar, saying "hey" to each group as they passed, the cooks the rowdiest bunch as usual. Only one of the cooks spoke English, so Spanish phrases filled the air.

Domingo always worried about hiring illegals but he liked the versatility they gave him: paying them in cash, no taxes, no social security, and it was easy to fire them. Just threaten to expose them to the police.

Finishing his sandwich, he wondered what to do, so he went to his office to call Detective Billy Harris. Harris had told him to call with any new information. Well, thanks to Brianna's call, he had a new question: was he going to be arrested by the Feds?

First, he noticed he had two missed calls: one from Harris, one from Joey Lingua's wife, Molly.

Harris: *Mr. Domingo---Detective Harris---got some news. The Feds are looking for you. Can't say much---National Security. Call me back.*
Molly: *Johnny, Joey's been picked up by the Feds. I can't get to him. I think you need to get outta town. This is real bad.*

Domingo tried to sort it out: *What the fuck is goin' on? Shit, I rented a place to Morel, but I know nothin' about the murders. Harris knows all that stuff. I told him everything I know. Why'd he flip me over to the Feds?*

He tried to get Harris, but he didn't pick up his cell. Who else could he call? He tried Molly Lingua.

Molly?..... Yeah…I'm okay…I heard your message….yeah…but out of town, why?....I'm not understanding any of this shit….News said Palmer Morel did it, now it's me?......I can call my lawyer….Wadda ya mean, that won't help….So, if they get me, I'll put up bail…They can't do that….What the hell's the Patriot Act? Shit, I'm a fuckin' patriot…The Feds can do that? ….No trial?.....Wadda mean, no charges?.....Okay, okay, I hear ya….Jesus, I don't have anywhere to go….Listen, I'm leavin' the restaurant now…right, they know I work here…right, but it sounds like I can't go nowhere….Yeah, call me you hear anything. I got my cell phone…..Thanks….. See yah.

29

Ghosts

Brad Hollofield, Cat Gallaher, Mrs. Morel and Palmer Morel waited inside the Welcome House for the first "Ghastly Ghosts" trolley of the evening, scheduled for 7 pm.

Palmer had arrived with his mom first, parked Andi's Kia in the lot and waited outside. Soon, Cat pulled her car to a stop along side his car. After a few hugs, Palmer introduced his mom and the group had walked inside the Center.

Now the arrival of the trolley sparked some new fear in Mrs. Morel. "All well and good, Palmer, you needing a job and meeting your friends, but what good can come from this? A little fun? Your dad's still dead. Your new girl is still dead. I don't see us doing anything about them," she ranted.

"Mom, settle down. I told you I got cemetery plots for them at Bonaventure. Being together now gives us a chance to talk, figure things out. See if we can have a memorial for dad and Andi or something. You can explain everything to Cat and Brad. Tell them about secret dad's background. All that stuff. They'll understand more. Maybe you three can get some plan going, I don't know."

"We could've just talked at the motel. Much easier. This is just crazy."

Cat tried to soothe her, "Mrs. Morel, Palmer needs a job. This will help him. He's got only little cash left. You don't have much money either, do you? While we're here will find him a place to stay, another apartment some place."

Mrs. Morel would have none of it, "Humph, someone got him that place in the cemetery crypt. That was really great, huh. What's next? You get him a real grave?"

Brad had to laugh at that one. "Listen, Palmer's mom. You got some spunk. You remind me of my mom back in North Carolina. She full of sass like you. Palmer's lucky to have you, but he's got us too. Come on. Give us a chance. We'll get through this."

***

Near the Myrtle Beach exit, Trooper Niquist's prediction came true. Looking out his rearview mirror he watched as a patrol car got closer and closer behind them, it's red and blues blazing. Niquist looked over at Melty, "I told you, sir, We're fuckin' toast."

"Let me handle them. No problem."

Niquist pulled onto the berm and waited. *This should be good,* he thought.

The patrolman strolled over to the driver's side window. "Hello, officers. I'm Officer Narada stationed over at Florence. We got an APB on you issued out of Wake Township up in Carolina. Says you guys are headed down to Charleston, that right?"

Melty piped up, "Yes, officer. Max Melty here. My driver Ken Niquist."

"Well, I had a tough time catchin' up to you. Guess you were goin' pretty fast, huh?"

"Not too fast, were you Ken? Hope we ain't in no trouble?"

"No, sir. Just got a message for you the Feds sent about you and the Hollofield case, some murder up there in Pittsboro at the jail? That why you driving south today?"

"Yes, sir" said Melty. "Had a tip about our boy Hollofield being down in Charleston."

"Well, the message the Feds have sent says forget about Hollofield. Says they got it all wrapped up down there in Savannah. Some terrorists done it. They have two arrests and two deaths."

"Forget Hollofield they say? You sure? Can you send that message here to our computer?"

Narada frowned, "Okay, sir, but you should have it on your computer already. You got your system turned off?"

Niquist interrupted, "Yes, officer. Colonel Melty doesn't like to interrupt his trips with "hogwash" he gets from the computer, so I turned it off."

Glaring at Melty, Narada admonished, "Might be nice if you kept in touch with your computer messages, Colonel Melty. Might save us from chasing after you, right? Good day gentlemen."

***

"Gentlemen, ladies," said the thin, British actor and history buff. "I'm George Arthur, your guide for an evening of scary scenes and frightful facts."

Palmer and the others smiled. "Good meeting you, George. I'm Palmer Morel, this is my mom, Joanna Morel, my friend, Coach Brad

Hollofield, and my other good friend, Cat Gallaher. Hope you don't mind them being here while you train me this evening."

Arthur smiled in the British manner, reserved but warm, "Not at all, Palmer. They can grab a seat near the back of the trolley as I introduce you to the best role of your life, the part of a ghostly barker on this converted, ghastly trolley bus!"

While Palmer remained at the front of the trolley, the rest made their way to the back, deciding to sit at the very end of the trolley.

Palmer had a few questions. "George, you're wearing a costume, sort of a dark Dracula outfit with a hairpiece; at least I think that hair's not your's, right?"

"Very perceptive, Palmer, very perceptive. Yes, we are required to develop our own scary attire. Doesn't have to be homemade perfection or expensive, just some clothing that sets you apart, makes you spooky."

"Uh, should I check with anyone, let them know what I'm doing? Do they reimburse my money for the outfit?"

"Yes and no. Do check with our dear Mrs. Lingua first and, no, she will not pay for your attire, though you can take it off your income tax, I guess."

Palmer said, "Then, I'll give it some thought, come up with a persona."

"Quite right, but I'd wait a day or two. I will see how you do at the talking part here on-board; then I'll give a report to Mrs. Lingua. And after all that, if you're hired permanently, you may establish a glorious get-up."

Watching as George prepared the microphone and opened the front door as the tourists started to arrive, Palmer asked, "And my script? Do you have an extra, one that I can borrow?"

"Oh, yes, yes, I forgot. Here is the script. Stick to it with little variation. You can add your personality, of course, maybe throw in a few jokes, but essentially we try to give the tourists the same spiel no matter which ghost trolley they ride. And, of course, you'll be reading it today for part of our trip so I can check your diction, your loudness, your personality, your charisma, that is, if you have any," George quipped.

Palmer nodded, "Before we start, can I sit down and read through it?"

"Oh, of course, of course. Go ahead sit in the front, over there in that seat directly behind the driver. Not too many folks like to sit there because they can't see too well stuffed away. But you'll do nicely, won't you?"

Palmer looked at the small space and wondered, "I guess."

He sat down, George adjusted his black, shiny wig and his red tie, and the first family of tourists arrived, clomping up the steps. It was 6:45. The tour would start in 15 minutes.

***

"Hey, guys! I've got 15 minutes till show time," yelled an excited Morel when he bounced to the back of the trolley to see how everyone was getting along. He was a little worried about his mom and Cat, since mom called Cat "a slut" once or twice. But they seem to be chatting up a storm and Cat was showing her photos of TJ.

"See, Palmer. I told you I would love Cat like a daughter," Mrs. Morel said, a twinkle in her eye.

"She's a real dynamo, your mom. Told me what an average day back in Sedalia is like for her. Couldn't believe it! Breakfast, cleaning, gardening, a walk, shopping, volunteering at the kindergarten, exercising at the gym, another walk, dinner, out to a movie and back home in time to watch "Big Brother"!"

"Wait," said Palmer. "You left something out. Mom. Don't you still watch "The Young and the Restless" every day?"

"My only vice," his mom replied.

"How's your script?" asked Brad. "Easy?"

"Take a look." Palmer handed the script to Brad.

"Hmmm. Okay." Then in a deeper voice, "Here's what it says: *Travel the timeless paths of poetry and pain. Discover the morbid delights of ghastly death and decay. Learn Savannah's ghostly secrets. Come with me. Ha, Ha, Ha, Ha, Ha!*"

"Whoa, Brad! That's good," said Cat. "Maybe you should sign up too. You sounded a lot like Dracula."

***

Emily said to Clint, "Well, we need to wrap this up."

"I agree," Mr. York said, "but there's some loose ends: the funeral, the Bonaventure burial, maybe contact Morel. He's paid for the cremations, the burial plots. You know he's a victim, too. Pathetic."

Mrs. York nodded, "Yes, yes, but what can we say? Palmer will suspect something if we say too much. Will he go running to the police, to Congress, to the goddam president? Best just play the grieving parents."

"Yes. We've seen Andi's diary, her photographs, some un-sent letters to Morel. He was a bit older, but still…"

Emily said, "Yes, I know. There was a deep attachment there, for both sides. I was surprised when I saw that poem Morel wrote to Andi….real feeling….real depth….very surprising."

"Yes, yes, a real love affair and at the beginning I really wanted to kill Palmer, almost did. But I can't tell him that…I can't tell him about Andi's primary reason for meeting up with him."

Emily said, "Andi had a change of heart."

"Yes."

"And she was getting out of military service."

Clint answered again, "Yes."

"Is that why, you know, why the father…."

Clint added, "…James Morel."

"Yes, James Morel was contacted. St. Julian …."

Clint finished, "…called James. Yes. They had worked together for many years. Getting rid of loose ends."

"What? Getting a call from St. Julian, then performing ….?"

Clint continued, "Of course. And James Morel always answered the call."

"Yes, but not as a killar……."

Clint said, "….Andi was his first time."

"Did he know….realize that Andi had decided to drop out…that Andi really loved Palmer?"

Clint said, "I don't think so. Andi had just met him. He had driven down from Chapel Hill. It didn't matter. He was prepared for it. Focussed. He had three guns in a gym bag, carried the "baby" around with him, liked it."

Emily said, "So you think…after that crazy phone call, Andi reacted, screamed, and James Morel…."

Clint whispered, "…reacted."

"He felt it was time to carry it out….?"

Clint said, "I think so, but, you know, according to Lingua, James had been sleeping, woke up very surprised, and …."

Emily said, "…reacted out of fear, out of….?"

"…necessity."

"Yes, but he didn't see Lingua…."

Clint finished, "…and didn't realize Joey was sexually attacking Andi. He just…."

Emily finished, "…fired the baby. Did his duty."

Clint added, "Yes….that was it."

Emily guessed, "One shot…."

Clint finshed, "…yes, and our Andi died."

Emily teared up, "I miss our Andi so much……"

Clint added, "…….so very much."

30

Bonaventure Goodbyes

Sara drove down to Savannah in her Karmann Ghia, bringing TJ with her. The Ghia impressed TJ so much. It was small. It was cute. It was a convertible. He had to have one!

For the entire ride down from Deerington, the top was down and TJ was buckled in securely in the backseat with his bag full of toy trains. He took big gulps of air like a dog, his senses pricked by flavors, aromas and the tactile ecstasy of wind on his face and arms. He was almost giddy with pleasure.

The little car rounded the turns on Bonaventure Road, finally reaching the main gate of the cemetery. Going past the gates, Sara turned into the parking lot, still dotted from the rain from the previous day.

She extracted TJ from his seat, got him his bag of trains, set him on the grass and immediately her cell phone rang.

Palmer: Sara, we're back along the edge of the Wilmington River. Start down one of the roads and I'll see you coming.

Sara: Okay, I'll pack up TJ again. He's eager to see you. Can you hear him? (Palmer heard TJ's happy cries of "Daddy, Daddy.")

Palmer: Whoa! I sure can. Can't wait!

Sara and TJ got back in the Chia, headed around and through the huge live oaks, the slight wing blowing the Spanish moss on the limbs. It was an exotic setting and Sara had often visited Bonaventure when she was an undergraduate at Savannah State.

Now she could see Palmer waving. She waved back and TJ just shrieked, his voice spreading through the cemetery, one might say awakening the dead.

The small group of mourners had gathered in a semi-circle around the two graves as she pulled up near the crossroads.

With his toy trains in tow, TJ took off, running through the grass and into Palmer's arms, his little body squirming with delight.

Sara followed at a slower gait, her eyes watching for roots as she took a more graceful path winding around the various gravestones.

Palmer and Cat came over first, giving her a group hug. Then Brad enveloped her in his strong arms. She noticed the three older visitors, all looking visibly shaken.

Palmer introduced his tired mom, Joanna, and then brought the older couple over, too. The Yorks seemed greatly affected by their daughter's death, both with dried tears on their cheeks.

No police officers, FBI agents nor military special ops personnel were present, just eight American citizens there to pay homage to Andrea York and James Morel.

Sara's artist's eye caught the poetic images on the large gravestones: James Morel's had an engraving of day lilies, his favorite flowers; Andrea York's had an engraving of a jazz dancer, her favorite activity.

Even TJ got quiet when Palmer stepped forward to read the elegy:

>These two sprightly spirits
>
>never mingled their thoughts,
>
>before they did depart.
>
>
>
>For one was old-school,
>
>faithful, sharp,
>
>the other youthful
>
>pensive, tart.

That their souls

shall rest here

in this shady nook

befits their nature

their vision

their acting parts.

Andi and James

from different eras

will remain together here,

forever in our hearts.

As soon as Palmer finished, his little son ran over to the two graves. He pulled out two toy trains from his bag. One toy train, Thomas the Tank Engine, he placed on James Morel's grave. The other engine, Emily, he placed on Andi's grave.

Then, TJ turned around a gave his dad a big smile.

Also by Larry Rochelle

Novels

PSYCHED	DIXIE SLOTS
LOCKS	PLAZA BLUES
MILITIA	TEN MILE CREEK
TRACES	MURDER ON 15/501
THE NUNNERY	BONAVENTURE
PLAZA LINE	

Poetry

SIREN SORCERY

PISTOL-WHIPPED

GHOSTLY EMBERS

MOODY BLUE

I GOT DA EVER LOVIN KC BLUES

ARROW

HOME SCHOOLED

BURNT COFFEE

DUST DEVILS

Larry Rochelle

Growing up in Toledo's West Side, Rochelle learned tennis and golf at Ottawa and Jermain Parks. His mother, Claire, often took him to Sigmond Sanger Library where he started off with sports fiction, particularly Claire Bee novels. "I loved those action stories, and later I collected quite a few first editions of his books." Also credited for his literary bent are the Notre Dame nuns who taught at Toledo Gesu School. "Each one of them in the early grades read to us in class. What excitement!"

Here are some moments in his writing career.

DANCE WITH THE PONY 2001 "I spent five years in Cincinnati and got a feel for its schizophrenia. My book explores the hypocrisy of its conservative veneer." PONY won the 2004 CITY BEAT AWARD for best novel about Cincinnati.

CRACKED CRYSTALS 2003 "A combination of Kansas City and St. Marys (sic, no apostrophe), Kansas, with a little magic and the occult thrown in for mysterious seasoning." CRACKED was a finalist for an EPPIE in 2004.

GHOSTLY EMBERS 2005 "I was in a nostalgic mood while I wrote these poems. I picked the 1950s in Toledo so I could explore some of my memories of grade school and high school." GHOSTLY EMBERS won an EPPIE for poetry in 2006.

BLUE ICE 2005 "I've been fascinated by the mob in Kansas City ever since I followed the Senate assassination committee in the late 1970s. The mob has had a direct line from Chicago, to KC, to Dallas. BLUE ICE uses a mob motif to explore a fictional Thanksgiving mystery in KC and in the Paola area." BLUE ICE was nominated for an EPPIE in 2006.

HOME SCHOOLED 2007 "I played golf in Osawatomie, Ks and have written poems about this area. Mostly the area is beautiful and full of history. I've tried to capture some of the feelings of the area." HOME SCHOOLED won the KANSAS POETRY BOOK AWARD for 2007.

Rochelle has had a frenetic writing career so far, publishing 22 books since 2001. And, as he likes to demonstrate, he has written all of these books using just one finger. "Yep, I'm a one-finger typist. I started that way in high school. We had a very old Underwood typewriter and there was no way I could type normally on it. The keys took too much power to push down. So...you want to see me type now?"

His new 2011 novel, BONAVENTURE, is set in Savannah.